"This sounds like a joke."

"I have no idea what you're talking about. I didn't put any ad in the paper."

"I just happen to have a copy with me. I printed it out because I wanted to show some people here at work. I think it's cute that you're acting shy about it now."

She showed it to me. Beneath a picture of me there was this:

Jack Grammar would never try to fondle your butt during a slow dance.

Jack Grammar is a gentleman, owns his own tux,

and has superb taste in corsages.

Jack Grammar is looking for a prom date. Could it be you?

E-mail MyNewPromDate@yahoo.com

When my shift was over, I sat down and pulled up the web browser and typed in the address.

Dear MyNewPromDate@yahoo.com:

It is with deep gratitude that I thank you, benevolent anonymous benefactor, for the intelligent and humane personal ad, which I'm sure will prove to be a pivotal event in the narrative of my maturation.

Your humble servant,

Jack Grammar

P.S. I will poke your eyes out with a coat hanger.

D0011601

Perkins County Schools
Media Center

OTHER BOOKS YOU MAY ENJOY

Alt Ed	Catherine Atkins
The Cheat	Amy Koss
How My Private, Personal Journal Became a Bestseller	Julia DeVillers
LBD	Grace Dent
Notes from a Liar and Her Dog	Gennifer Choldenko
S.A.S.S.: Westminster Abby	Micol Ostow
This Lullaby	Sarah Dessen
Thwonk	Joan Bauer

24 girls in 7 days

ALEX BRADLEY

speak

An Imprint of Penguin Group (USA) Inc.

SPEAK

Published by the Penguin Group

Penguin Group (USA), Inc., 345 Hudson Street, New York, New York 10014, U.S.A.

Penguin Group (Canada), 90 Eglinton Avenue East, Suite 700, Toronto,
Ontario, Canada M4P 2Y3 (a division of Pearson Penguin Canada Inc.)

Penguin Books Ltd, 80 Strand, London WC2R 0RL, England

Penguin Ireland, 25 St Stephen's Green, Dublin 2, Ireland
(a division of Penguin Books Ltd)

Penguin Group (Australia), 250 Camberwell Road, Camberwell,
Victoria 3124, Australia (a division of Pearson Australia Group Pty Ltd)

Penguin Books India Pvt Ltd, 11 Community Centre, Panchsheel Park,
New Delhi - 110 017, India

Penguin Group (NZ), Cnr Airborne and Rosedale Roads, Albany,
Auckland 1310, New Zealand (a division of Pearson New Zealand Ltd)

Penguin Books (South Africa) (Pty) Ltd, 24 Sturdee Avenue, Rosebank,
Johannesburg 2196, South Africa

Registered Offices: Penguin Books Ltd, 80 Strand, London WC2R 0RL, England

First published in the United States of America by Dutton Books,
a member of Penguin Group (USA) Inc., 2005
Published by Speak, an imprint of Penguin Group (USA) Inc., 2006

 Produced by Alloy Entertainment
151 West 26th Street
New York, New York 10001

3 5 7 9 10 8 6 4 .

Copyright © Alloy Entertainment and Jeremy Jackson, 2005
All rights reserved

CIP Data is available.

Speak ISBN 0-14-240543-4

Printed in the United States of America

Except in the United States of America, this book is sold subject to the condition that
it shall not, by way of trade or otherwise, be lent, re-sold, hired out, or otherwise
circulated without the publisher's prior consent in any form of binding or cover
other than that in which it is published and without a similar condition
including this condition being imposed on the subsequent purchaser.

The publisher does not have any control over and does not assume
any responsibility for author or third-party Web sites or their content.

part **1**

chapter 1

I FEEL, TO BE HONEST, like a man in a space suit. In space. Because despite the fact that I'm in the middle of a stupid overcrowded narrow hallway surrounded by masses of my excessively chatty peers freshly released from fifth period, I can hear nothing but my own breath and I feel very separate and very far from my own planet and it seems like there's no gravity. I might float away. There also seem to be stars twinkling at the edges of my vision. Where the heck am I headed? Who sent me on this insane quest?

And to top it off, my hands are numb. My hands are very numb, but I keep moving down the hall, trudging onward, and now I can see the doorway from which Pamela Brown will appear at any moment. Oh, for the love of all that's good and holy. Oh, for the love of frick.

My comrades sent me on this mission moments ago with semihelpful encouragement. "Luke," Percy said, gripping my shoulders too tightly and using his best Darth Vader voice, "this is your *destiny*."

"I'm not Luke," I said.

"Don't quibble, my son," he said, still in character.

"Besides," I added, "Luke didn't get the girl. And the girl was his sister anyway."

Natalie nodded. "He's got a point," she said.

"Er . . . uh . . ." Percy-Darth said.

Natalie winked at me. "We believe in you, Jack," she said.

"But I don't . . ." I protested. "I'm not up for this. I just don't think it's me. It's not something I can do. It's not something I've ever done. It's not something I ever *will* do. I'm not good at it. Honestly."

She clasped my shoulders and smiled, looking me right in the eyes, and instead of responding to my last-minute blabbering—the kind of excuses I'd been spewing all week, the kind of excuses she had talked me through ten times already—she simply turned me in the right direction and gave me a little push. Thus I was shot into outer space. I was off.

My legs and feet seem to be working well, even without my direct involvement. Now I'm passing under the banner advertising the prom, the thing itself, the night of nights, my date with fate. XANADU, the banner reads. Or, as we've been calling it: Xanadon't, Xanadope, Xanaduped, and, the twin favorites, Xanadoohickey and Xanathingamadoo.

Most of the students have already left Pamela's classroom, but where is she? I have a sudden vision of her hiding just inside the doorway, back flat against the wall, waiting for me to pass so she can escape, but the reality of the situation is that Pamela wouldn't hide from me because she doesn't know who I am. Unless, of course, she has a remarkably good memory and recalls the one time we talked last year:

Scene—lunchroom

Time—12:32 P.M.

Setup—One Jack Grammar is waiting in line for the only Coke machine in the entire flipping school when he realizes a certain Pamela Brown is standing behind him. Stunned into silence by the fact of her proximity, he's surprised by a tap on the shoulder.

PAMELA: Do you know what time it is?

Now, let's hit the pause button, shall we, and consider our hero's mind. John Alexander Grammar. Aka "Jack." Aka "the Jackster." Aka me. The question being posed to him is simple: Does he know the time? Well, does he? Yes. Therefore this should be simple, right? He is, after all, Jack Grammar, and he does, after all, have more AP credits than is possible without special permission from Dean of Students Canton Schramm. He also has a watch. He should, in all honesty, be able to answer the question before him with not only excellent accuracy, but also humor, ease, wit, and boyish charm.

JACK (*looks at watch*): 12:32 . . . About. I think?

PAMELA: Thanks.

Not only does Jack not know what to say as a follow-up to Pamela's expression of gratitude, but he suddenly finds himself at the front of the vending-machine line, and after shakily feeding his coins into the slot, he bumps the Diet Coke button.

In other words, if Pamela Brown remembers anything about me, it's that I drink girl soda.

Then suddenly there she is. She comes out of the classroom alone, holding her books to her chest, schoolgirl-style. (Well, she is a schoolgirl, I suppose, so that makes sense.) I marvel: even in doing something so simple as leaving a classroom, she oozes grace. She tours with a ballet company every summer, after all. But—uh-oh and crap—she's taking a most alarming course through the crowded hallway: she's going all the way over to the opposite wall, whereas I've been sticking close to *this* wall, and that means I'm in trouble. Here we are at the moment of truth. Here I am, the spaceman in deep space, having finally spotted the green and lovely planet that is my destination—my hope, my dream, my personal springtime—and suddenly that planet is jumping from its expected orbit and I'm going to have to waste precious rocket fuel in a last-second effort to bring myself in. And if I miss this landing, I'll fly right past the planet, careening on into the inky black void of space, likely never to return. . . . A dateless spaceman . . .

To my credit, I veer heroically across the hall.

Twenty feet, ten feet, five feet . . . I bring myself closer, and suddenly even walking is difficult, requiring all my concentration. Even breathing seems to be strangely complicated right now. . . .

This is absurd.

I think about the three possible opening lines that I had prepared for this moment. The lines that I spent all week writing, all last night rehearsing. The lines that are written on the palm of my left hand. But my beautiful and appropriate lines are gone from my head. There are no words in me.

I open my palm a little, but I stop because Pamela is looking at me. I am blocking her path.

No time to read my lines! Must improvise! Alert! Alert! Improvisational chitchat, now!

"Hee," I say. Hee? Did I just say hee?

"Hey," she says, but she's not sure about this whole thing.

Her eyes are these giant green globes—twin planets. Her hair, a golden cascade. Even her braces are like tiny jewels. . . .

Then she says a thing that blows my mind: "You're Jack, aren't you?"

How can I flub this one? "Yeah," I say. "You're . . . Pamela?"

She nods, says, "You have a little dog, don't you?"

"Oh, him. I mean, yeah. He's a Jack Russell terrier. If you like that kind of thing."

What? *If you like that kind of thing?*

She smiles. "I think I saw you guys playing Frisbee down in Riverside Park," she says.

"Yeah, that would be us. We're going to make the Olympics in 2008."

"I like a man with a plan."

What's this? What is this most unusual sensation? Am I being flirted with? By Pamela Brown?

"I've never seen you in the park," I say. (Lie.)

"I play tennis there."

"Oh, really? That's cool." (She plays Tuesdays, Thursdays, and Saturdays, four thirty to five forty-five, weather permitting, preferably on court 3, with her friend Reba. She uses a Prince racket, Wilson tennis balls, Diadora court shoes. Backhands are her strength, serves her weakness. She doesn't sweat.)

"I guess," she says.

I look at my watch. I tap it. Why did I just do that?

"Tennis!" I bark, as if I just now heard what she said twelve seconds ago. "So what's that like?"

"What's what like?"

"Tennis."

She's got a blank look.

"It's fun," she says. "You've never played tennis?"

"Uh, no. Uh, just slightly. I mean, I was on the team in junior high." Her blank look turns into a puzzled one.

"Hey!" I say, as if something brilliant has occurred to me. "Are you interested in this whole Xanadu thing? Because I realize we don't really know each other, but I was just thinking that it would be a good opportunity to do just that. I mean, if you don't already have plans."

I can see her shoulders—her ballerina shoulders—getting ready to shrug me off. There's a *pre*-shrug forming.

"Hm, *prom* . . ." she says, drawing the word out and considering it as if it were something she'd heard of but never really thought seriously about. She nods. "That sounds kinda cool."

"I don't know if it'll be cool per se. But it'll be a thing."

"A thing?"

"A thing? Did I just say 'a thing'?"

"Uh-huh."

"What did I mean?" I say.

"What do you mean, what did you mean?" she says.

"Ha-ha!" I say. Forced laughter. "It's just that, well. A fine time will be had by all. That sort of thing. And, well—And, so—And, and—I guess—Well, I mean . . ."

The great spirit of doubt is clouding her face. I have to rally fast.

"Well, we being seniors and all," I explain, "it's our last chance for us to go in for this sort of stuff. And the fantastic transgenic forces of springtime are surging around us. And who can pass up an opportunity to eat some cheap cake and all? And punch! Do you like punch?"

Her eyes have narrowed, and she's angled her shoulders away from me, and for a brief moment I see her look past me, at someone or something behind me.

"You're a senior?" she asks.

"Yeah . . ." I say. What's she getting at?

"I thought you were, like, a sophomore."

"Well, I *was,*" I say. "I *used* to be. . . ."

"Hm," she says. "Weird."

"But should I call you or something, or . . ."

"It's just," she says, "that I don't think I'm going to the prom."

And she walks away.

chapter 2

AN HOUR LATER, WHEN THE final bell rang, I was the first out of the classroom. I race-walked down the center of the hallway, weaving and dodging as needed, and then took the stairs two at a time. "Dictionary, dictionary, dictionary . . ." I muttered.

I got to my locker and jammed my textbooks in my backpack and then knelt and started digging in the pile of papers and notebooks that had accumulated at the bottom of my locker since the beginning of the year. "Dictionary . . ." I said. The hallway was filling up around me.

I knew I had a little paperback dictionary in there, but I couldn't find it. Then I got reckless and started digging with both hands and that's what set off the landslide, which was big enough to knock me off balance for a second. I tottered to the side and just then Adrian Swift opened her locker—right next to mine—and I banged my head on her locker door.

"Frictionary!" I said.

"Jack!" she said. "I'm sorry!" She knelt by me.

"My fault," I said, rubbing the side of my head.

"That was really loud," she said.

"I'm fine," I said. "Just a flesh wound." And at that moment I saw my dictionary, unearthed by the landslide. "Gotta go," I said, grabbing the book.

"Are you sure you're okay?" she asked, but by the time her question was out, I had already grabbed my dictionary, crammed everything else back into my locker, and was making a swift retreat. I didn't want to talk to Adrian right now. I'd had my awkward girl encounter of the day already. Plus I never wanted to talk to Adrian, actually—I knew she liked me and *she* knew I knew she liked me and when she had asked me to the Sadie Hawkins dance last year, I had told her I had rickets, which was just such an embarrassing lie that we both blushed simultaneously and she apologized for asking me and ever since then we had tried not to make eye contact, which was especially challenging now that our lockers were next to each other and we shared calculus class.

I walked out of the school, flipping through the dictionary.

Minutes later we were driving to Coralville in Percy's little station wagon. I was in back, slumping. I had no energy for posture.

"Let's list things that are sadder than Jack's love life," Percy said.

"In other words, a very short list," Natalie said.

"Exactly," Percy said.

"I'm not participating," I said.

"Good," Percy said. "Item number one: little kids getting lost in supermarkets."

"Oh, that's sad," Natalie said.

"Item number two," Percy continued, "my grandmother losing her glasses on top of her head."

"Very, very sad," Natalie said.

"Item number three," Percy said, "the fact that Bert and Ernie are still in the closet after all these years."

"Tragic," Natalie said.

We were crossing the river on Park Road and I looked at the water. The sun was sparkling on the river, and normally it was a sight that moved me, but today it seemed far away, or filtered, like I wasn't observing the thing itself, but a painting of the thing. Or a photograph of a painting of the thing, observed in a mirror, backward.

"Do you guys know what 'transgenic' means?" I asked.

"Transgenic?" Percy said. "I think I have that CD."

Natalie said, "Doesn't it have something to do with how all the continents used to be one big continent?"

She was thinking of Pangaea.

"No," I said.

"Why are you giving us vocabulary drills when we're trying to rib you about your romantic incompetence?" Percy asked. "Because if you think you're going to derail the conversation, you're wrong."

"That's right," Natalie said.

The fantastic transgenic forces of springtime. I'd said that exact phrase to Pamela. I'd said other stuff that was stupid, but for some reason this was the one that bothered me. No wonder she'd been scared off. If I was that freaky when I was simply asking her to the prom, why would she think I would be any less freaky when we were at the prom itself?

Transgenic had turned out to have something to do with chromosomes and genes. It was one of those annoying words that when you looked it up, its definition contained words whose meanings you had to look up, too.

"The thing is," I said, "I think she sort of said yes and then changed her answer to no."

In the front seat Natalie turned around and lowered her sunglasses—those rhinestone-studded sunglasses that would look wrong on anyone else. She stared right at me.

"She did what?" she asked.

"I think she said yes at first. I'm positive. I'm mostly positive."

"And she changed her mind?" Natalie asked.

"Yeah."

"Jeezum crow, Jack," Percy said. "You transformed a 'yes' into a 'no' in one conversation?"

"I guess," I said.

"That's amazing," Percy said. "That's like some kinda superpower or something."

Natalie said, "But what happened between the time she said yes and the time she said no?"

I shrugged. *Transgenic.* "I said how much fun it would be to eat some cheap cake."

"Eat cake!" Percy exclaimed. *"Eat cake?"*

"And she said she thought I was a sophomore. She thought I was younger."

"If she wants you to be younger," Percy said, "be younger. Tell her you're a *third* grader if that's what it takes."

"Don't listen to him," Natalie said.

"Why shouldn't he listen to me? Compare my love life to his and tell me he can't learn a few things from me."

"Yes," Natalie said, "but the problem with you, Percy, is that you're hollow."

"I don't want to lie to anybody," I said.

"Listen to me, Jack," Natalie said. "Pamela Brown is not for you. You're better than her."

"And I don't want to graduate from high school having only kissed one girl."

"Hollow?" Percy said.

"She looks like an ostrich," Natalie said.

"And I'm not going to go to the prom stag," I said. "That's worse than going with my sister."

"Hollow, eh . . ." Percy said.

"You could go with *my* sister," Natalie said.

"Your sister's like twelve," I said.

"Thirteen."

"Do it!" Percy said. "Junior high is where the *action* is. The satis*faction*."

"You know she's in love with you," Natalie said.

"Do it!"

"She writes your name with her glitter pen inside her notebooks."

"Do it!"

"She'll be getting breasts soon. . . ."

"Maybe even before the prom . . ." Percy said.

I sighed. We were out in Coralville now, at one end of the strip, and the stoplights and fast-food chains and mini-malls stretched before us. The hole in Percy's muffler must have been getting bigger because it was louder today than I remembered it, and I could feel it pulsing between my temples.

"Bridget and Jackie!" Percy taunted, braking for a stoplight.

Natalie unbuckled herself and turned around and wriggled her way into the backseat with me. She was all arms and legs and blond hair, and she had a whole oddly appealing klutzy thing going on. She reached back into the front seat and retrieved her iced coffee, which she then offered me.

"Drink," she said. "Be happy."

I took a sip, but it was too sweet and coffee wasn't really my thing anyway.

"I give up," I said.

"I don't hear that," Natalie said.

"I do," Percy said.

We turned right, into a big parking lot, and drove around to the back side of the plaza. Percy parked and got out and Natalie rolled down her window and we sat there. It was a breezy day, and it was warm in the car.

"You've got the holy trinity of what a girl wants," she said. "Cute, smart, funny. I don't think you realize that."

"But even if what you say *is* true, what good has it done me? I can't get a date for the prom. I'm weeks away from graduating from high school without being deflowered."

"Well, flowers come and flowers go. It's not a big deal."

"Flowers don't come, they just go," I said. "Or they go nowhere."

"Tell me," she said, "you may not have gotten a date yet, but how many girls have you asked?"

"One," I said.

"Well, that just means it's time to ask number two."

I crossed my arms and sighed. "Point taken. But I reserve the right to be glum for forty-eight hours."

"Twenty-four."

"Glum for twenty-four, plus moody for twelve."

"Agreed."

We shook hands.

"But I'm not sure I have the energy to ask someone else out," I said. "It took everything in me to do what I did today."

"I know. But you *did* it. It didn't kill you."

"It killed me a little bit," I said.

Natalie took my hand and rubbed it and then she said, "Jack, Jack, Jack." Then she put her head on my shoulder. We sat there quietly for a minute, and I felt a little better than I had ten minutes ago. Then I reached up and touched the sore spot on the side of my head where I'd hit Adrian's locker.

At that moment the passenger door opened and Percy's grandmother poked her head in—her freshly washed and styled globe of hair.

"Hi, you kids back there!" she said.

Natalie sat up. "Hello, Mrs. Kowalski," Natalie and I chimed.

She lowered herself into the seat and Percy closed her door for her.

"You look lovely, Mrs. Kowalski," Natalie said.

"Oh," she said, waving her off. "I look like I look and that's all I'm gonna say about that!"

Percy got in the driver's seat and started the car. "The topic of the moment," he told his grandmother, "is that Jack can't get a date to the prom."

Mrs. Kowalski turned her head and looked at me. She was a woman with a permanent smile.

"Oh," she said, "then put out the word because this boy, he's some kind of catch!"

chapter 3

THE NEXT DAY—SATURDAY—just before noon, I took my lunch break. The crowds in the mall were horrible, so I turned heel and went right back into the Barnes & Noble. I bought a muffin that looked like survival food, and I scouted around for the quietest corner of the store I could find. Ironically, that was the children's section—my section.

As I ate at a kid-sized table, I pulled interesting titles off the shelves and read them. The muffin crumbled into dust as I picked at it, so I abandoned it and kept reading. It was the same load of kiddie literature as usual, then I found a book called *Andalusia*. It was a picture book with huge pages. I opened it and it was beautiful—saturated, magical watercolors of the underwater world in a stream.

I am a baby, the little trout said.

Next page: *My world is underwater.*

Next page: *But there are others like me.* And the picture showed a wide-angle view of all kinds of fish and crayfish and bugs and turtles in the stream, and I found myself cheering inside. Yay! There are others like her!

The table moved a little bit and I looked up and I'd been joined by Felicia Deatsch.

"Hi, Jack," she said.

She worked in the café but always managed to wander through my section and bother me.

"How was your muffin?" she asked.

"Spanktacular," I said.

She laughed. It was a snorting kind of laugh.

"But you didn't eat the whole thing . . ." she said.

I looked at the pile of muffin dust. I wasn't hungry today. I hadn't been hungry last night either.

I shrugged and tapped my watch. "Gotta go back to work in two minutes," I said. She was always tough to get rid of.

"Oh, heck, I'm working right now," she said, as if to prove how rebellious she was.

"Working hard or hardly working?" I asked, hoping to bore her with tired jokes.

But she laughed as if she'd never heard it before.

"That's funny," she said.

"In a way."

She was smiling like she had a secret. "I saw your ad," she said.

"My ad."

"Your ad."

"Ad?" I said.

"Online."

"My ad online?" I asked.

"I did."

"Hm," I said.

Now she was smiling coyly, like we were kids talking about something dirty.

"The thing is," I said, "I have no idea what you're talking about."

"Yes, you do," she said, smiling more. She thought I was flirting with her.

"I really don't."

"You do."

"I don't."

"You're just playing hard to get," she said.

"That's ridiculous. I'm not hard to get at all."

"I think it's cute."

"Let's be clear here," I said. "What exactly are we talking about?"

"Prom?" she said. "Have you ever heard of prom?"

"Sure, and?"

"Your ad online. In the *City High Weekly.*"

"Online?"

"Yeah."

"*City High Weekly?*" I said. Our illustrious school newspaper.

"Yeah."

"This sounds like a joke."

"I've already e-mailed you. So you don't have to give me an official answer right now. I just wanted to touch base with you, though, since we've always been good friends. And so I hope I'll be hearing from you."

"I just checked my e-mail this morning. I have no idea what you're talking about. I didn't put any ad in the paper."

"I just happen to have a copy with me. I printed it out

because I wanted to show some people here at work. I think it's cute that you're acting shy about it now."

She showed it to me. Beneath a picture of me there was this:

> Jack Grammar would never try to fondle your butt during a slow dance.
> Jack Grammar is a gentleman, owns his own tux,
> and has superb taste in corsages.
> Jack Grammar is looking for a prom date. Could it be you?

> E-mail MyNewPromDate@yahoo.com

"Is it true?" Felicia asked.

"Is what true?" I said, still staring at the ad.

"That you own your own tux."

The ad couldn't be real. It looked made up. It was like it was written by ten-year-old boys.

"Jack?" Felicia said.

But wait. Wait, wait, wait. This wasn't real. It *couldn't* be. After the whole Pamela catastrophe yesterday, there was no way that even a cruel God would throw something like this at me.

"Jack?"

I waved the ad. I waved it furiously. I didn't know what to say. "This is a joke!" I yelped.

Felicia smiled. She thought I was acting.

I put the paper down. I pointed to the words. "Tell me this is a joke. You wrote this. You printed this out."

"Are you kidding me?" she said.

"Damn it, I don't think it's funny. It's really mean."

"But . . ." she said.

"Did you make it up?"

"No. I swear."

"It was online? In the paper?"

"Yes. Last night."

"I didn't place this ad," I said.

I looked at the ad again. It wasn't even a good picture. It was my school picture from last year—the only picture in the history of me in which I looked cross-eyed.

"If you didn't write it," Felicia asked, "then who did?"

Perkins County Schools
Media Center

chapter 4

WHEN MY SHIFT WAS OVER, I put my time sheet on the assistant manager's desk. I looked at his computer. I thought about it: he wouldn't come into his office. He was never in his office. He was always up front. He wouldn't know.

I sat down and pulled up the web browser and typed in the address.

"Hey!" someone said behind me.

I jumped up from the computer, banging my thigh on the keyboard tray. But it was just Felicia, turning in her time sheet.

"You're bad," she said. "You're not supposed to be in here."

But she agreed to act as my lookout, keeping an eye on the hallway.

It didn't take long. *Click click*, there it was. There was the ad, online, for all the world to see. It was in the personal ad section of the school newspaper, which just made it all the more embarrassing and conspicuous because normally when you signed on to the home page of the newspaper, there was a little banner that said ———> Current Personal Listings (0)! <———, because no idiot in the history of City High had ever been so dumb as to place an actual personal ad in the school paper. But today the banner said ———> Current Personal Listings (1)! <———. Right up there at the top of the page. To make matters worse, nearly half the school checked the website on Friday night or Saturday because that's when the video clips from that stupid Friday exit poll thing appeared. So hundreds of kids had seen that ———> Current Personal Listings (1)! <——— since last night.

I clicked on the e-mail link in the ad, and the e-mail program automatically opened a window and addressed the e-mail. So I wrote to MyNewPromDate@yahoo.com. I put my heart into it. I put my soul into it. I put my advanced vocabulary and creativity and wit into it. And I put my frustrations into it—from yesterday and from my years of unrequited pining for Pamela and from the dawning knowledge that I would not be attending this year's prom with anyone and would be laughed at for my ridiculous personal ad. I wrote:

Dear MyNewPromDate@yahoo.com:
    It is with deep gratitude that I thank you, benevolent anonymous benefactor, for the intelligent and humane personal ad, which I'm sure will prove to be a pivotal event in the narrative of my maturation.

                    Your humble servant,
                    Jack Grammar

P.S. I will poke your eyes out with a coat hanger.

I sent the e-mail and the computer chimed, giving me a feeling of satisfaction. Felicia was looking at me in awe from the doorway and then she said, "Uh, do you realize you're on Mr. Corbin's computer and you just sent that e-mail from his account. . . ."

I looked at the computer screen. The picture of me in the online ad was smiling right back at me. *Ha-ha!* the digitized, cross-eyed me was saying. *Transgenic! The fantastic transgenic forces of springtime! You, sir, are an idiot.*

Outside, I called Dan on my cell phone. He was working at the other end of the mall—at Best Buy—and he often gave me a ride home on Saturday. We got off work at the same time.

"Jackie, I'm already in the car and I'm already on the way and in about forty seconds I'm going to come around the corner and you'll see me," he reported.

That he called me Jackie was one of the reasons I liked him.

"Ten-four," I said.

"Hey," he said, "can you hear my car stereo from where you are?"

I listened. "No. Don't think so."

"Let me turn it up. How 'bout now?"

"Oh, yeah," I lied. I knew it would make him happy. "I do. That's cool."

"I got that new amp booster I was talking about! That's why you can hear me. Can you tell what song I'm playing?"

I named the song and he laughed at the triumph of his massive car stereo. Of course, he didn't realize that I wasn't hearing the song from halfway around the mall, but through the telephone. He wasn't the smartest nut on the tree, true, but that's how Natalie liked her boys. She and Dan had been dating since just after he'd graduated from West High last year. Of course, all of Natalie's boys were very, very pretty, and Dan was no exception. He also got along with everyone, and when you were with him, you generally felt better than you had before he arrived.

I got in his car, and a little bit of my sour mood dissolved immediately. By the time we were up on the interstate and zooming back to Iowa City, I'd already told him about the stupid personal ad, and then I showed him the copy that Felicia had let me keep and he read it and started screaming, "This sucks! This sucks! This sucks!"

I could only nod. It felt good to have him screaming on my behalf.

"This sucks so much!" he said.

"I know," I said.

"I mean, who would do this to you?"

"I don't know."

"Who hates you so much they would do this? How could anyone hate Jackie?"

"Maybe they think it's funny," I said. "Maybe it's someone who doesn't hate me. They just think it's funny."

"Oh," Dan said, as if something had occurred to him. We were pulling off onto the Dubuque Street ramp. "Uh-oh," he said.

"Uh-oh what?" I asked.

"What if it was Natalie?" he said.

His people instincts were sometimes dead-on, and as soon as he said it, it sounded right. It clicked. Or half clicked. The ad had been a little crude for Natalie to write by herself. It had the fingerprints of some classless jackass on it, some brainless jerk. . . .

"And Percy . . ." I said. "Natalie and Percy. My best friends."

·   ·   ·

I left messages on Natalie's cell phone. I used every expletive I could think of. Then I made some up, too. Then I kept leaving messages where I would just hold my phone in front of my stereo and let a whole song play. As far as I was concerned, she and Percy were guilty until proven innocent.

Percy got off easier. I knew he was out with Penelope and he didn't have a cell phone. I didn't even bother calling his home phone because his grandparents would answer and want to talk with me about how school was going and ask yet again when I was going to come by to sell those pecans for the French Club fund-raiser—which I hadn't done in two years.

For lack of anything better or more productive to do, I decided to write Natalie some harassing e-mails. I got online. I had a random e-mail from someone I didn't recognize: FancyPants242@hotmail.com:

Hey there, cowboy. Just what is it about prom that makes every-one crazy? I was in Walgreens yesterday and I swear they actually had a magazine called *Prom Hair*. You dig? I mean, this particular piece of journalism bragged that it contained not 100, but 101 fabulous floral hairstyles. Yippie ki-yi-yo! Also, there was a whole article devoted to prom hats. Well, I say let them have their fantabulous baby's breath hats. I don't need no stinkin' hat. And my hair is just fine with its Supercuts walk-in special, thank you. And why, oh why would a person go to the prom, say, when they could just skip the whole thing and go to the Pancake Haus instead, where you can partake of those chocolate-chip pancakes

with the whipped-cream smiles? Ever had those? Damn, those
are some happy pancakes.

What the heck was going on? Who the frick was FancyPants?
And why was she writing to my personal e-mail? The stupid
online ad listed that MyNewPromDate e-mail. But FancyPants
had obviously seen that ad and then looked me up in the school
directory.

Then a weird thought occurred to me: what, I considered, if
the ad actually *worked*? What if the girls flocked to me?

No, no. That was ridiculous. This FancyPants was a fluke. Or
a fake. It was just another part of the joke. Ha-ha, good one,
Natalie. I fell for it for a little bit.

I decided to respond, though. Because what if she was real?
I liked what she was saying. It was a darn good e-mail. What
if she was my soul mate? What *if*? I re-read the e-mail. I wanted to know who this was. Was she asking me to the prom? Did
I know her? Should I just ask her right now if she'd go with
me?

I had to play along, even if it was a joke:

Dear Miss (Ms.? Dr.? Prof.? Ambassador?) FancyPants:
I dig, man. I dig. Talk to me.

                                                            JG

I heard footsteps in the attic above my room. Dad's little cubby-
hole office was up there. I closed my laptop, left my room, and
went up the attic stairs. The stairs were steep and wooden and
unfinished. Our house was one of those big Victorians tucked

away at the end of Iowa Avenue on a short, private street with big trees.

To get to Dad's office, you had to walk across the unfinished part of the attic.

"I hear someone coming . . ." Dad said before I got to his door.

"It's just your son," I said.

"Son!" Dad exclaimed. "Don't speak to me of sons! I have no son!"

I stopped in the doorway.

"Oh, *that* son," Dad said.

"How long have you been grading papers?" I asked. "You're loony." He taught English at the university.

"Oh, since about dawn, I guess," he said. "I drank nine cups of instant cappuccino." He held up the empty box to prove it.

"I don't know if that's something we need to brag about," I said.

"Or tell Mom about," Dad said. He looked at his watch. "Is it time to go over to Hetta's?" We were having a cookout at my sister's house.

"Pretty soon," I said.

He was looking at me as I scanned the titles on the bookshelf.

"You don't usually visit me in my office," he said. "What's up?"

"Nothing," I said. "Long day at the office."

"You're pregnant again, *aren't* you?" he said. It was one of his favorite jokes.

"Do you think we could go over to Hetta's a little early?" I asked. I figured being surrounded by my family would distract me from the disasters of today and yesterday.

"Sure."

"Who'd you take to your senior prom?" I said.

He took off his reading glasses. "You know who I took to my prom."

Of course I did.

"That's right, you took Mom."

"She said 'no' the first two times I asked her."

"She did?"

"And then the third time she said that if no one asked her in the next two days, she would think about it."

"I didn't know that."

"And the fourth time she said she would think about it. Then she said 'okay.'"

"How'd that all make you feel?"

"Like crap, my boy. Like crap. But that's the point of prom, I think. Last time I checked."

At Hetta's house Dad and I came around the house to the backyard. Mom, who'd been here all afternoon, met us at the gate. Across the yard Hetta and my other sister, Jane, were setting the picnic tables. Their husbands, Ben and Jerry (no kidding), were hovering over the grill. And the collective brood of these two couples—my two nieces and two nephews—was chasing Pat the wiener dog. But when the kids saw me, the oldest of them, Perry, pointed at me and ordered an attack. Thus I was brought down by the hands of infants, who clung and later piled onto me with remarkable determination, eventually pinning me on the lawn. During this process, the bag of hot-dog buns I was carrying was irrevocably flattened to approximately the thickness of a wallet.

Minutes later I was inside and I washed my hands and looked in the bathroom mirror and caught a glimpse of myself in which I seemed slightly cross-eyed, which just reminded me of the stupid ad. I went to the kitchen and helped Hetta and Jane with the food and tried very hard not to think about the ad or Pamela or anything, but that was kind of like that dumb thing where someone tells you not to picture a purple elephant or whatever and, of course, you picture a purple elephant. Then Jane chimed in.

"So when I got my haircut Wednesday, Natalie told me you were going to ask someone to the prom," she said. Natalie worked at a salon, sweeping the floor and answering the phone. "So how'd that go?"

"It didn't," I lied. "I'm waiting for a special girl to ask *me*."

Hetta and Jane laughed.

"Oh my God," Hetta said. "I just remembered how we used to dress up as kids and make Jack be our prom date. Do you remember that, Jack? You must have been too young to remember."

No. I remembered. I remembered them wearing their Easter dresses and a lot of Mom's old costume jewelry and explaining the rules about the corsages—which we made from flowers in our own yard—and the rules about how to ask them to dance. I did everything they told me to. Yes, I might have been only four or five, but I remembered it all: the dimmed lights, the records spinning on the record player by the window, the decorations of crepe paper and construction-paper stars hanging from the chandelier in the family room. And how one time they'd gotten permission to get out all the old Christmas lights and they strung them all over the place and it was like a whole different world in there. I remembered the punch of equal parts 7UP and Hi-C.

And the way they made me ring the doorbell and then wait at the bottom of the stairs while they came down over and over again. It was a game we played a lot for about a year, and perhaps it was the root of my current problems because the fact was that I loved it. I loved the idea that prom was a night of magic and possibility. I believed in prom before most boys had even heard of it, and I still believed. Not that I'd ever admitted that to anyone.

I should have learned long ago that my life wasn't going to be any kind of fairy tale. Wasn't that the lesson of junior high: to realize that life wouldn't be a fairy tale but some kind of extremely ill-conceived, sloppily produced, and usually pretty boring reality-television show? Yes, I knew better. I knew the prom was just a dance organized by a bunch of pep-squad busybodies with GPAs somewhere in the low 2s. But in all honesty, in my most private self—the part of me that talked to my dog and still made a wish on the first star I saw at night—I still believed in prom.

If this prom slipped by without conjuring up some kind of magic—some romantic miracle—I was pretty sure that it would only be a sign of things to come or, more precisely, a sign of *nothing* to come.

I looked at the package of kid-flattened hot-dog buns on the counter and it was all perfectly clear to me at the moment: that's me. And who wants flattened hot-dog buns? No one.

I was about to answer Hetta and admit that, in fact, I did *vaguely* remember the fabled prom enactments of our childhood, but I was suddenly kidney-punched by Perry.

"Ow!" I said.

Hetta and Jane laughed.

"I have two girlfriends!" Perry shouted.

"Congratulations," I said, rubbing my back. "Do you want a medal?"

"Okay," he said.

"No, I don't have a real medal to give you, I just meant . . ." But I didn't feel like explaining sarcasm to him. He was five.

That's right, five: my own nephew, less than one-third my age, had *two* girlfriends, whereas I had never even had one.

chapter 5

NATALIE'S DAD'S HOUSE WAS ONE of those big postmodern boxes built into the bluff above the river. It was the kind of house that screamed, "I'm a big-shot lawyer," which was exactly what Mr. Sharpe was. The house was very vertical. It had four floors. You could either park at the bottom of the bluff and enter on the ground floor, or you could drive to the top of the hill and enter on the top floor. During the weekends and summers Natalie stayed with her dad. On weekdays she was at her mother's house, which was exactly two doors down, at the top of the hill. Her mother's house was very horizontal.

I pulled in at the bottom of the house and called Natalie from my cell. "We're at the top," she said. "Drive up here. The doors are locked down there."

"Wait, what do you mean 'we'?"

"Percy's here."

"I thought he was out with Penelope."

"He was, but he wanted to be here for this."

"Tell him I'm going to poke his eyes out."

"Yeah, we got your e-mail. Just come up."

So I started the car back up and turned out onto Rocky Shore Drive and then went up the hill and parked in the circle drive at the top of the house. Inside, Natalie and Percy were sitting in the expansive formal living room. The entire western wall was made of glass, and it looked out at the bend in the river. The last stains of the sunset were fading above the horizon.

"Please join us, Mr. Grammar," Natalie said.

"I am *not* sitting down." It felt good just to be contrary.

"Relax, Mustafa," Percy said.

"In fact," I added, "I'm not sitting down until you apologize to me and *then* tell me the strange reasoning process behind this whole prom-ad joke."

"Tell me what you want to drink," Natalie said.

"I'm not thirsty. My righteous indignation has quenched my thirst!"

"Listen," Natalie said, "if you want to blame somebody, blame Percy's grandma."

"All right, then," I said. "Damn you, Mrs. Kowalski, wherever you are!"

Natalie said, "Remember when we told her you were looking for a prom date and she said we should put out the word?"

"Sort of," I said.

"Well, we did," she said.

"But did she go out and write a stupid ad and put it online?"

They didn't answer.

"Did she?" I asked. "No! Because she's not an idiot! She's not a wanker!"

"Wanker?" Percy said. "What's a wanker?"

"I don't know," I said, "but I know that in movies, that's what English people call their friends when they're acting like idiots."

"We're sorry," said Natalie.

"You don't sound very sorry. It's all very well for you two to laugh at me. You both have relationships and standing dates every weekend and you're going to prom, so I can see how this joke ad seems very funny to you."

"It is a little funny, if you think about it," Percy said.

"I've been thinking about it all day!" I shouted. I was pacing. I stopped. "I don't believe this," I said. "I have to lie down now." I stretched out on the carpet and looked at the ceiling.

"We were just thinking of what's best for you," Natalie said.

"We had an agreement! I was going to be gloomy for a day and a half and then I was going to ask someone else."

"See, we didn't believe that," Percy said. "Your track record with these kinds of things didn't give us much confidence."

I got up from the floor and sat in an overstuffed chair. "That doesn't give you a right to meddle."

"We believe," Natalie said, "that this will be instructional for you. We believe this will be good for you. We did this because we thought it was something you had to go through."

"Everyone's going to laugh at it. Laugh at *me,* actually. No one will take the ad seriously."

"We have almost forty responses so far," Natalie said. "Serious responses." Then she sipped her seltzer. Percy looked at her.

"Forty-five, actually," he said.

I looked out the window at the waning sunset. Then I looked at my hands. I wasn't sure how to feel at this particular moment. There was a numbness inside me where thirty seconds ago had been anger. Something was going to happen to me. Something was going on.

"Forty-five . . . ?" I finally asked.

Natalie said, "And we expect more."

"See, Jack," Percy said. "You gotta go with it. You've gotta let it happen."

"But tell me the truth," I said. "I mean really tell me the truth. Did you guys do this as a joke?"

They looked at each other.

"Primarily," Natalie said.

"We thought it was a hoot," Percy said.

"Ha-ha," I said. "Hardy frickin' har."

"But the point is," Natalie said, "it's turned into something real."

"I don't even think I *know* forty girls . . ." I said.

"We're sort of worried about you, bud," Percy said. "We're not going to be around for you next year. We're all headed in different directions. You're going to be on your own. You have to go through with this thing, you have to learn how to be your own guy."

I nodded. I did tend to cling to them. They were the center of my life. I'd never been to a party without one of them. I shame-lessly tried to infiltrate their dates every weekend so I wouldn't have to hole up in my room alone. I ate lunch with them every day at school. Having such close friends meant I didn't have to do the hard work of talking to other people, making new friends, asking girls out. I was scared of being without them.

"It's okay to be a little scared," Natalie said. Leave it to her to read my mind.

"I'm *not* scared," I countered, though the way it came out—like a little kid saying he's not sleepy—simply confirmed the opposite. "I'm still mad at you guys and I . . . I . . . I'm very, very thirsty."

"Well," I explained to Bridget, Natalie's little sister, "my best relationship lasted thirty-five minutes."

Bridget and I were down on the first floor, playing pinball. I was on left flipper, she was on right. Percy had left to resume his evening with Penelope. Natalie was upstairs making popcorn.

"Let me clarify," I said. "My *only* relationship . . ."

"Was that the airport girl?" Bridget asked.

I looked at her. "Does Natalie tell you everything?" I asked.

The ball went right past my flipper.

"Hey, ace," she said, "that was your ball."

"Sorry," I said.

"So you met this girl on a layover . . ." she prompted.

"Yeah. We shared an Au Bon Pain cookie and a Coke."

"What size?"

"Oh, I'd say she was about five-six."

"I meant the Coke, dingus."

"Medium."

"Mm-hm," Bridget said, as if the size of the soda revealed the secrets of my character.

"And then she kissed me—"

"On the cheek?"

"On the lips, and then she got on her flight."

"Where to?"

"It was Delta flight 213. To San Francisco. Gate B12."

"Where were you going?"

"To Biloxi. To see my uncle Dewp."

"Dewp?"

"Dewey, but everyone calls him Dewp."

"And what was your girlfriend's name?"

I paused.

"Jack?" she prompted.

"The funny thing is," I said, "I never asked her name."

I could hear Natalie coming down the stairs. We hit the triple multiplier and then the ball went into the Spinergizer. Then Bridget hit a wicked bank shot that flattened the final bonus peg.

"White magic!" the pinball machine said.

"Ah, man! Bridget, you're the best," I said.

"The best what?" she asked.

"Chase the lightning!" the machine commanded.

"We're going to set a high score here," I said.

"The best *what*?" she repeated.

"You're my best sister," Natalie said, munching popcorn beside me, "but only by default."

As I drove back across Iowa City in the family Camry, it started to rain. It was a gentle spring rain that arrived without fanfare and I could tell that it was going to stick around all night. The streets gleamed and I rolled down the window just a little bit so I could smell the rain.

At home I pulled into the garage and turned off the car. I waited for the garage door to close and then I sat there for a few moments in the silence. I felt tired. It had been a long day. Being pissed off at my best friends had worn me out. Maybe they were right that I should go out with some of the girls who responded to my ad. Maybe this was the magic of prom, turning a horrible joke into something good. The prom was in exactly one week. I wondered: what would I be doing one week from this moment?

chapter 6

I FELT FOGGY AND GLUM after I got home from Natalie's. A late-night run was what I needed, so I laced up my shoes and went back outside. The street in front of the house was hushed. It was still raining, and the rain made a gentle sound on the leaves. I ran west, toward downtown.

Yes, I was totally annoyed with Percy and Natalie. They'd created this situation without thinking it through. But mainly I was frustrated with myself. Why had it come to this? Why was I such a tremendous freak?

I ran past Old Capitol—its gold dome illuminated by floodlights—then headed downhill toward the river. Even though it was a Saturday night, the town was quiet; even the college kids were inside. I felt like I had the town to myself, and I liked it. Maybe that was my problem. Maybe I was just a born loner. I was like one of those monkeys on the Discovery Channel who voluntarily separates himself from the clan and spends his days sitting alone on some rocks somewhere, scratching himself. By the time I was thirty, I would probably live in a shack in the woods and my only contact with living creatures would come from my conversations with squirrels and birds, who would eat right out of my hand and perch on my head. To fill this role, I would have to grow a bushy beard, of course, and the locals would need to come up with some kind of nickname for me. The Squirrel Man. The Shack Dweller. The Transgenic Loser.

"Jack?"

I snapped out of my dreary fantasy. I was running along the river path now and another runner was beside me.

"Hi . . ." I said. She looked familiar, but I couldn't place her.

"It's Lucy," she said. "From the Firefly Club."

"Oh, hey!" Last summer we saw each other running after dark all the time. Eventually she started running along with me. We called it the Firefly Club—we only came out after dark. Lucy was barely five feet tall, and her hair was pulled back in the standard runner's ponytail. She was so extremely cute—like an anime girl hero—I never understood why she wanted to run with me.

"Isn't it great that it's finally warm enough to run at night again?" she asked.

"It's so neat," I said. "Like fresh ketchup."

"Fresh ketchup?" she said. She laughed.

"I mean, um, how great ketchup can be, you know, when you just open a fresh bottle."

"I suppose," Lucy said. "Never noticed it before."

Neither had I. Fresh ketchup? It had just popped out of my mouth.

Lucy talked about her senior year at the university. I tried to listen, but I was too nervous, the way I was around almost all girls. I just kept thinking about what I should be saying in response to what she was saying and then I was thinking about how to be a good listener and with all of this thinking going on, I lost track of what she was saying and suddenly I snapped out of it as she said, "I mean, do you really think I should apply for that kind of thing?"

"Oh, yeah," I said. "Totally. I guess. I mean, I . . . One time I was . . . I mean, you have to assess yourself or . . . find yourself. Together. Or both. For that sort of thing."

"That's one way to put it," she said, puzzled.

We ran in silence.

"You seem a bit down," she said after a while. We'd run all the way to the city park and had just turned around to head home.

"Oh, no, I'm really happy," I said.

"You're a hard guy to figure out."

I did a running shrug. "I'm just thinking about stuff."

"Like what?"

"Books," I said. It wasn't true.

"Are you a big reader?" she asked. "What books?"

"Uh, *Watership Down.*"

"I've never read that."

"Me either," I admitted.

"But you're thinking about it?"

"Yeah," I said. "I'm thinking about reading it." I was glad it was dark out so she couldn't see me blush.

"Oh," she said. "Well, more power to you. And the bunnies."

After that exchange I had to escape, so I told her I needed to deviate from our normal route because I wanted to run a few hills on Dubuque Street. So we parted ways.

Hills, schmills. I ran straight home.

Luckily I slept like a dead man. I woke up at noon, which was impressively late, even for me. I felt fantastic. I took a quick shower and then headed downstairs. And it was on the landing that I remembered everything—the prom, Percy and Natalie, forty girls. . . . My mood changed immediately.

I rummaged in the refrigerator with great frustration.

"There's nothing to eat here, people!" I yelled into the quiet house.

Only after several seconds did Mom answer from a distant room: "There's plenty! I just went shopping yesterday!"

"There's nothing!" I replied. "No breakfasty stuff."

Mom padded into the kitchen, eyeing me impatiently over the rim of her reading glasses.

"Look," Mom said, "here's that yogurt you wanted me to buy."

"I refuse to admit that I ever asked you to buy me yogurt. Yogurt has estrogen in it."

"That's not true."

"I don't want yogurt."

"Well, there are those bagels you like in the freezer."

I made gagging sounds.

"You picked them out yourself, remember?" Mom asked.

"Hm . . ." I said, rubbing my chin like I was trying hard to remember.

"Well, there's fruit," Mom said.

"Fruit!" I exclaimed. "Fruit is the reproductive organs of plants!"

Mom rolled her eyes and turned. "Isn't it a little late for breakfast anyway?" she said as she left the room.

"It's never too late for breakfast," I countered. "Ever!"

Flip trotted into the kitchen, stopped cold, and looked at me. "What're you lookin' at, peewee?" I said. He retreated. "I'll get you, my pretty," I called after him, "and your little dog, too!"

Mom came back in. "You're threatening the dog?" she said.

"He looked at me funny," I said. "Really funny."

"I'll make you an omelet," she said.

I went and hugged her and thanked her and said that an omelet sounded good but that I would just scramble some eggs for myself. She sat at the breakfast bar and took off her glasses. She smiled.

"We've always called you our no-maintenance kid," she said, watching me crack an egg. "We don't even have to cook for you."

"I don't think I'm no-maintenance. I just think that after raising Hetta and Jane, you guys are lazy. You didn't even ask me where I was last night. You're a bad, bad parent."

"So, where were you?" Mom asked.

"At Natalie's. Then I went for a run."

"See, we never have to worry about you."

"Well, start worrying because things are going to change right"—I paused and looked at my watch—"*now.*"

"I don't believe you," she said. "You're a wonderful kid and pretty soon you'll be a wonderful adult."

"Okay, but does *being* wonderful mean your *life* is wonderful?"

"Eventually," she said.

"I'll take your word for that."

With my eggs steaming on my plate, I walked into the living room and opened up one of the cabinets. There was a whole series of photo albums here, all labeled clearly and arranged in chronological order. I pulled out the one I was looking for. I sat cross-legged on the carpet and opened the album. There was one picture I wanted to see. Just one.

I found it. It was more than thirty years old, but the image was clear and crisp. It was a photograph of my parents at their prom, and I hadn't looked at it in a long time. They looked young, even with their weird hippie haircuts. They looked even younger than me. But you could also tell that they somehow belonged together. They didn't know it yet, but they'd be together for the rest of their lives. You could tell they had a bond.

My phone started ringing upstairs. I did an impressive charge up the stairs, sliding skillfully around the landing in my socks, and got the phone right before my voice mail would have picked it up. It was Natalie.

"Dairy Queen," she said. "Fifteen minutes. How's that sound?"

"Sounds like breakfast," I said.

We sat at the sticky picnic table between the gas station and the Dairy Queen parking lot. This was perhaps one of the least attractive places in Iowa City for one to enjoy ice cream. Market Street was usually a busy street, and Dubuque Street, fifty feet away, was even worse.

"Down to business," Natalie said after finishing her Dilly Bar.

"I thought this was a social call," I said.

"Wake up and face reality," Natalie said.

Percy was spooning down into the depths of his Butterfinger Blizzard. Bridget was licking a cone of soft serve like mine.

"We're here to talk about your ad," Natalie said.

I turned to Bridget. "Did you know this ice-cream run was a trick to get me to talk about that stuff?" I asked her.

"I know nothing," she said. I doubted that, though.

"Okay," I said. "Go ahead."

"One hundred and forty-eight," Natalie said.

"One hundred forty-eight what?" I asked.

"Responses to your ad."

"One forty-nine," Percy said without looking up from his ice cream.

"Oh, that's right," Natalie said. "One came in at the last moment."

I opened my mouth to say something. Then closed it. Then opened it again.

"One forty-nine?" I said slowly. "I don't believe you. How is that even remotely possible?"

"I know," Natalie said. "It's pretty amazing, right? An embarrassment of riches."

"No," Percy said. "An embarrassment of bitches."

"Yuck," Natalie said. "Don't say that."

"Sorry," he said. He looked at Bridget. "Sorry, Bridget."

"'Sokay," she said.

"I don't understand," I said. "Why would so many girls respond?"

"Don't play coy," Natalie said. "Your picture alone was enough to get that many responses."

"That isn't true. I look cross-eyed. Plus the stuff you guys wrote was horrible."

"Don't blame me," Natalie said. "Percy wrote it."

Percy nodded.

"But I *would* try to fondle my date's butt," I said. "That's who I am."

"No, you wouldn't," Natalie said. "You're just being contrary. You're a sought-after guy now, Jack. Just accept it."

"Just like that?" I said. "All of a sudden?" Natalie just smiled. "And I don't even own a tux," I said.

"Don't you have one of those T-shirts that looks like a tux?" Percy asked.

"I haven't worn that in years."

"Anyhoo," Natalie said, trying to move us along, "we're going to make it easier for you." She pulled a few pieces of paper from her bag. "We spent the morning sorting through the responses and selecting some girls. A lot of the responses weren't even from our school. And some were from college girls. Most of them you probably don't know. We did some research, though, some background checks. We called around. These four are a good start."

"What do you mean a good start?"

"You can start by going out with them and deciding if you want to go to the prom with one of them."

Why did this sound like *work* all of a sudden? Why did it sound like a job I didn't want to do?

"You're way ahead of yourself," I said. "I didn't agree yet to go out with anyone."

Natalie sighed. "So you want us to tell them all to leave you alone? You want us to disappoint almost a hundred and fifty girls?"

"Yes," I said. I tried to picture what a hundred and fifty people would look like, all standing together, frowning. I couldn't.

"Maybe," Percy said, "we should select a certain number and Jack could go out with all of them and then pick one. Set it up from the start like that, tell all the girls the rules, make it more exciting."

"That sounds good," Natalie said. "That's a great idea."

"Hello?" I said. "I said I haven't agreed."

"How many should we choose?" Natalie said to Percy. "Twenty?"

"Hm," Percy said. "More."

"Twenty-four," Bridget said. "Because there are seven days until the prom and so it'd be twenty-four girls in seven days, which has a nice ring to it."

"Hey!" I said to her. "Don't help them. Be on my side. My side!"

"Twenty-four seven," Percy said. "I love it."

"Listen! How am I supposed to choose from twenty-four girls in one week?"

"Oh, so you're agreeing?" Natalie asked.

"I'm just asking."

"Look," she said, "you'll start with these four. They already know there's competition. They'll contact you to arrange for their dates. As of fifteen minutes ago, they now have your phone numbers, address, e-mail address, and class schedule. They'll come to you. We've also forwarded their responses to the ad and any personal info to your e-mail. And here are hard copies of their responses, along with photos. Some of them submitted photos."

I leafed through the pile. I didn't know these girls. Well, I knew *of* one.

"For our part," Natalie continued, "we'll keep sorting through the responses we already have—plus any new ones that come in—and we'll send them your way until we get a total list of twenty-four."

"We'll call it 'the List,'" Percy said.

"Very clever," Natalie said.

"With a capital L," he clarified.

"Well, I'm still not agreeing."

"A hundred and fifty girls, Jack," Natalie said. "They like you, they really, really like you. Think about it. I've been trying to tell you how great you are and how you should ask more girls out and now here's proof that you're a catch."

"You're a super-catch," Percy said. "I wish I were a super-catch."

I looked at the printouts again. I felt my lips curling into an involuntary smile. I tried to force myself to look serious. This was serious business.

"Did you weed out Felicia Deatsch?" I asked.

"Yes," Natalie said.

"What about FancyPants?" I said.

"Who?" Natalie said.

"FancyPants. Someone named FancyPants e-mailed me yesterday. I liked her. I don't see her here."

Natalie and Percy looked at each other. "I don't remember a FancyPants," Percy said.

"Me either," Natalie said.

"That's weird," I said.

"Of course, I suppose you can go out with someone who's not on the list. But it's at your own peril."

"Done!" Bridget announced, chewing the final stub of her cone.

My own cone, forgotten, was melting.

part **2**

chapter **7**

PERCY DROPPED ME OFF at the front of the house. I was in a sour mood and my ice-cream breakfast was gurgling in my stomach. As I walked to the door, I saw Mom gardening in the side yard. She was talking to someone. I poked my head around the shrubbery.

"There he is," Mom said when she saw me. Beside her was a girl I didn't recognize. Suddenly I wanted to flee. Who the heck was this girl?

"Jack, this is Melanie," Mom said. "She's here to see you."

"Hi, Melanie!" I said, like we were best friends. She was a lanky blonde with a smirky smile. She had on a T-shirt that said SNARKY. She was standing with her hands on her hips, and I got the immediate impression that she was the kind of girl who in fifth grade would have aimed for my groin during dodgeball.

"I'm on the list," she said.

"What list?" Mom said.

"Uh, the yearbook marketing planning list," I said.

"That's the one," Melanie said. She winked at me. I was pretty sure Mom saw it.

"Oh," Mom said. "Well, she's been very patient waiting for you. But you two kids can run along now."

"Yeah," Melanie said. "Let's go plan the heck out of that yearbook."

"Absolutely," I said.

"Let's plan until we turn blue," she said.

"Okay," I said.

"Let's plan like newlyweds."

Mom wiped her brow. "Why don't you work in Jack's room?" she suggested.

Melanie and I walked around the corner of the house.

"Your mom doesn't know?" Melanie asked.

"Shh," I said. "Let's go back by the garage."

"The garage? Classy."

"Look, I . . ."

"How about we just go to your room, like your mom said?" she asked.

As if I wasn't nervous enough already. And as if it wasn't embarrassing enough that my mother trusted me so completely that she had no reservations about me being alone in my room with a strange girl. Or maybe it wasn't so much a matter of trust as it was the fact that I'd never given my parents any reason to worry about me doing anything scandalous with girls in my room—or anywhere on the face of the planet, for that matter. The thought never crossed their minds that their little no-maintenance, wonderful Jack would touch a girl except in the event that the girl needed first aid.

In my room she closed the door.

"Now, let's see . . ." I said. "Okay. All right. Okay. Who are you?" I got out the printouts Natalie had given me. What was I supposed to do with this girl?

"Melanie Frankel."

"Melanie Frankel . . ." I said, searching for her response to the ad.

"You look bigger in person than in your picture," she said.

"I can't find nothin'," I said, focusing intently on the pages of paper. "I can't find a thing here."

She came over to me. "Don't worry about that stuff," she said. "Just talk to me."

"Okay," I said. "Sure. Do you go to City High?"

"West," she said.

"Okay," I said, nodding. "What year are you?"

"I'm a junior."

"Uh-huh, uh-huh. And what are your hobbies?"

She sat down on the floor, leaning against my bed. "Is this a college interview?" she asked.

"No, I . . . Well . . ."

She patted the floor. "Sit with me," she said.

"Okay," I said. "Sure. I can do that. That's not a problem."

I sat.

"Relax," she said.

"All right. Not a problem either."

"Now kiss me."

"Ha!"

She leaned toward me. Our lips touched.

"Whoa!" I said.

"What's the deal?"

I stood up.

"It's just that . . . that . . ."

"You're skittish."

"No, it's more like I'm just, or, I'm, uh, I'm . . ."

She cocked her head, as if she'd just realized something. "You're *shy,*" she said.

"It's just that I didn't get much sleep last night. Or something. I missed breakfast and I feel dizzy."

"For me," she said, "kissing is a litmus test. I can tell from kissing someone whether they like me."

"Yeah. Oh, yeah. I know what you mean."

"I'm scaring you," she said.

"It's all a bit abrupt," I said.

"You're pacing," she said.

I hadn't realized it. "Oh, this?" I said. "I'm just walking. I'm a big walker."

"I'll slow down," she said. "I'll be good. Scout's honor." She pointed to the window. "Do you ever sit out on the roof?"

"Sometimes," I said.

"Let's do it," she said.

I wasn't sure it was the best idea, but she opened the window and stepped out onto the roof. I went ahead and followed. The sun was filtering through the leaves and it was pleasant and secluded up there. But my legs were shaky. We sat down.

Something occurred to me.

"Are you FancyPants?" I asked.

"Am I who?" she said.

"FancyPants?"

"If you want me to be," she said.

"No: I mean, is your e-mail address FancyPants?"

"No."

Flip poked his head out my bedroom window. He barked a small bark. It was a pay-attention-to-me bark.

"He hates it when I get on the roof," I said. "It's like he thinks I'm going to jump off or something."

"Hm, little dog," she said, looking at him. "Cute." She turned back to me. "Well, have you ever?"

"Have I ever what?" I asked.

"Jumped."

"Jumped from here? That's crazy."

She scooted to the edge of the roof and looked down. "What is it," she said, "ten feet?"

"I don't know," I said.

She scooted back over to me.

"Listen," she said. "I like you. I can tell. Come to the prom with me, say yes right now, and I can guarantee you that you and I will have an entire week of fun. I don't even think you can imagine the kind of prom that we could have. I'll make you into a whole new you. I think, in fact, that you're a little scared of what we could do. But that's good. You *should* be a little scared."

"You don't even seem like the kind of girl who would care about prom."

"Then get used to surprises," she said.

And she stood up, walked to the edge of the roof, and jumped.

"Holy flapjacks!" I said. Flip, in a frenzy of excitement, hopped out of the window and began barking like mad at the disappeared girl. I stood up and walked closer to the edge of the roof. Melanie was walking away across the lawn. She didn't look back.

.   .   .

I just stood there on the roof, wondering what I'd gotten myself into. I scratched my neck and looked at Flip.

There was a knock at my bedroom door.

"Jack?" Mom called from the hallway. "I'm leaving two sodas out here for you guys. And some Goldfish."

"Thanks," I called in the window. But what if Melanie and I were in my room doing inappropriate things? Mom was feeding us without even asking us to open the door. That's how lame her son was: she needn't worry about that kind of stuff. I'd proven it already: I'd scared the girl away. I'd sent her over the edge.

I crawled back inside and closed the window and then realized Flip was still out there. He looked at me through the glass. I let him in. Then I heard someone open a soda can in the hallway. What the . . . ? Who was pilfering the sodas?

I opened the door and there stood Melanie, drinking a cold soda, calm as could be. She swallowed.

"So, what do you say?" she asked.

"I thought you . . ." I mumbled.

"Are we on or are we on?"

"We—on—or—and—or . . ."

She raised one eyebrow. "That was not impressive," she said. "So do I win? Are you mine for the week?"

The way she said it, with so much boldness or brashness or confidence or whatever it was, snapped me out of the shock of seeing her at my door again and made me wish that I were a different person and that I could at least think and talk straight in her presence and try the things I wanted to try. I'd lived here my whole life, but I wasn't even brave enough to jump off my own roof.

What came out of my mouth was: "I don't believe it's really the correct course for me to be pursuing at this time."

That puzzled her. "You're saying 'no'?" she asked.

I nodded.

"I thought you were a good one," she said, "but you turned out to be lame and boring, and I can tell that you're going to be lame and boring your whole life and that's not something I would wish on my worst enemy. So good luck with it."

She took another drink.

"And," she said, "I'm taking some Goldfish."

Then she left. With her soda. And some Goldfish.

chapter 8

I TRIED TO STUDY BUT couldn't focus. I tried to play PlayStation, but I was getting slaughtered. I felt disappointed. I felt strange. I felt like Melanie had bullied me. I felt scattered and . . . and . . . *not comfortable,* like she had come into my room and rearranged everything without my permission. Well, frick that. I didn't need that. I didn't need some half-baked scheme just to get a date to the prom. I didn't need this kind of abuse. I didn't need someone telling me I was lame and boring—I already knew that.

And was that my second kiss? That brief bit of lip touching that we'd shared before I'd freaked out? It was. It was my second kiss. I'd just doubled the number of girls I'd kissed, but the whole thing had left me really nervous and disappointed and basically sad. Wasn't kissing supposed to be a wonderful, natural, transcendental experience?

I wasn't going to play this game. So I sat with my laptop for the better part of the afternoon, composing several drafts of e-mails that could be forwarded to all the girls who responded to the personal ad. The point being to extract me from the present situation. Such as:

Dear Concerned Party:

Thanks for your interest in being my prom date. You're obviously a bodacious and wonderful person, and I've been looking forward to getting to know you. But I've just received the most unfortunate news. It seems that in my volunteer work with homeless blind immigrants, I have picked up a highly infectious strain of streptoneumiosis (whose symptoms include heaving, fainting, and bad breath) and am under doctor's orders to avoid all social contact for the next seven days. I'm not even allowed to talk on the phone. Fascist bootlicking doctors!

In other words, I can't go to the prom. This is disappointing, but I will get over it, and I have confidence that you will find a fantastic prom date.

Your friend,
Jack Grammar

Well, that wouldn't work, even if I made it more believable. After all, it wasn't as though I could skip school all week. My second attempt cited a death in the family. In my third attempt I claimed to be gay. Then finally I penned a beauty:

Dear _____:

I'm excited and pleased to announce my pre-engagement to Beatrice "B. B." Schipper-Bellingham of Winnetka, Illinois. She's a wonderful girl with inner grace, outer beauty, and exceptional intelligence. (As you may have heard, she won this year's

Jeopardy Teen Tournament. Her winning "question" in Final Jeopardy was: What are Aventine, Caelian, Capitoline, Esquiline, Palatine, Quirinal, and Viminal?)

I recognize that my pre-engagement comes at an awkward time and may disrupt your plans to escort me to the prom. Because of her modeling schedule, B.B. herself cannot attend my prom. And though B.B. understands that I should enjoy my own prom in the presence of a delightful friend such as yourself, her parents—both highly accomplished surgeons—have asked that I refrain from enjoying myself unless I am with their daughter (in which case they ask that I don't enjoy myself too much). Fascist bootlicking doctors!

In other words, I can't go to the prom. This is disappointing, but I will get over it, and I have confidence that you will find a fantastic prom date.

> Your friend,
> Jack Grammar
> (soon to be Jack Grammar-
>   Schipper-Bellingham)

Now, that one was nearly perfect. It was gorgeous, and I was proofreading it a final time when reality crept up on me. This fake engagement would keep me from attending the prom at all, which really wasn't what I wanted. What if, wonder of wonders, I did snag a date at the last minute without Natalie and Percy's help? Also, people would want to meet my fictitious fiancée. To extract myself from that mess, I'd have to concoct a fictitious breakup. That sounded like a lot of work.

Then again, if this prom had turned into such a headache, why go anyway? What was the big deal? It was just my hopes and dreams at stake, and they'd been dashed before, so surely they could be dashed again and I would continue breathing. And I was a hard worker and a darn good writer; I could construct credible documents to back myself out of the fake engagement without too much trouble.

There was a knock at my door, which was open. It was Mom again.

"Natalie's on the phone," she said.

"Oh," I said. "Thanks."

"Something wrong with your phone?" she asked, handing the phone over.

I told my mom that I'd been online all afternoon and that my cell phone battery must be dead. But really I'd turned all the phones off.

I put the phone up to my ear.

"Where have you been?" Natalie asked, before I even said hello.

"Here," I admitted.

"Oh, I get it," she said. "Not answering your phones. Very adult, Jack. Very mature."

"Well, they were ringing, and I didn't want to talk to whoever was calling me."

"I'm not going to let you back out of this thing. Not now."

I told her about Melanie Frankel. How she'd tried to kiss me and then jumped off a roof and then verbally abused me and stolen my Goldfish.

"Despite what you think," Natalie said, "kissing won't kill you. If you don't want to kiss anyone, why do you even want to go to the prom? And Melanie's very cute, so I know that's not a valid reason not to kiss her."

"But did you hear me? She jumped off the roof!"

"And?"

"And then she snuck back in and when I told her I wasn't interested, she got mean. She took my Goldfish! And . . . and . . . well, she jumped off the roof! Who *is* she?"

"It sounds to me like you're a little bit in love with her."

"I'm a little bit *not*," I said.

"You can say whatever you want. But I'm just calling to say that I'm behind this twenty-four/seven thing more than ever. I know it started as a joke, but the more I think about it, the more sense it makes to me. The more I think it will be good for you. *Great* for you."

"It's just that I don't think it will work," I said.

"But how do you know?" she asked. "I mean, you're a lot smarter than me, but I'm not sure this is something you know about. It's not an algebra equation. It doesn't have one correct answer. I think you have to go with it, let it teach you what it can."

"Damn you," I said.

"Why?"

"You're right."

"Of course I am," she said. "And I'm also calling to tell you that we've just let another girl through the screening process and I just e-mailed the info to you. So check it out ASAP because you've only got seven days. One down, twenty-three to go."

"I feel sick," I said.

"Bye, Jack."

I looked at my lovely fake engagement message for a good fifteen minutes, reading it over and over. "Okay," I said out loud. "Okay, okay, okay . . ." And I deleted the message, turned my cell phone and regular phone back on, and sat down.

I thought of Penny Gallagher, who I'd been in love with in

seventh grade. That's what I did: thought of a girl I hadn't seen in five years. She'd had a short boy's haircut and wore ratty jeans and sneakers when the other girls were getting into painted fingernails and the Old Navy psycho-slut look. Penny claimed her middle name was Radley, and she was the best whistler ever. She could do a really loud shrill whistle and a soft warbly whistle and anything in between. Sometimes in art class she would challenge me to come up with a song she couldn't whistle. She always won. I remembered standing at the big utility sink at the back of the art room, washing my hands, and she came up and showed me how because she was left-handed she got the drawing charcoal smeared all over the side of her hand and fingers. She soaped up and stood hip to hip with me and we washed our hands together—literally, with our four hands all slipping and soaping against each other—and we laughed and then we were rinsing our hands and we got quiet and I looked at her and she smiled and looked down and then looked back at me. That, I later realized, was the moment I was supposed to kiss her—even if it was just on the cheek—but I didn't. I didn't, didn't, didn't.

She and her family were going to move to Minneapolis the week after school got out and so I went to the art store and bought her the most expensive set of colored smudge-proof pencils I could afford and wrapped them in paper that I'd drawn tiny butterflies all over and I took the present to school every day for a week and finally I got the nerve to give it to her on the very last day, at the very last moment. I mumbled something, handed over the present, and walked away. I'd put a note inside the present and I didn't want to be around when she read it. In the note I said something about how it was sad she was leaving because I liked her more than anyone I'd ever known and that if she'd stayed, maybe we could have gone out together. I didn't see her again, but at the end of the summer she wrote me a letter asking why I hadn't told her that I liked her earlier. The letter was written in blue pen, but then the next sentence—the one after the one asking why I hadn't told her I liked her—was written with the colored pencils, with each letter a different color, in the order of a rainbow.

I liked you the whole time, she wrote.

So that was an opportunity missed. That was five years ago, and I'd learned by now that, in my world, opportunities like that didn't come along very often. And I didn't want to miss another. I just didn't. I owed it to Penny Gallagher. And I owed it to myself. That's what it came down to. That's when I decided.

24/7, here I come.

I got online to read the stuff Natalie had just e-mailed me. The new girl was named Callie Cunningham, and I recognized her name. She had e-mailed me a photograph of her hugging a very big and very happy golden retriever. Then she wrote:

Last night I dreamed I could play the piano. I can't, of course. Not in real life. But in this dream I sat at the keyboard and I could play like a virtuoso; not only that, but I was actually composing the music as I went, and it was exceptionally beautiful. The thing was, I felt like there was no boundary between me and the music. I was the music and the music was me and the piano was just the way we were united.

So, I realize this doesn't have anything to do with prom, but it was one of the best dreams I have ever had, and I wanted to tell you about it.

That was all. That was the extent of her ad. No arguments for why I should choose her. No posing. No boasts. No slang. And above all, no colon-parenthesis smiley faces. There was, however, an exceptionally impressive use of a semicolon.

Her response was by far more interesting than any of the ones Natalie had handed me this morning, so in my new spirit of taking advantage of good opportunities, I sent Callie an e-mail immediately.

> Dear Callie—
>
> For the record, I have recently been accused of being lame and boring. Redundant, I know. In the spirit of full disclosure, I feel obliged to tell you about this just so you don't get your hopes up.
>
> My dog, Flip, has told me he is interested in meeting your dog. He saw the picture you sent with your e-mail and he is very excited. He has asked me to attach a picture of him. He has never been accused of being lame and boring, but he did have fleas last year.
>
> Please send me your phone number so we can talk.
>
> Cheers,
>
> Jack

I attached a picture of Flip stretched out midair, sailing over an in-flight Frisbee. It was my favorite photo of him. It was something he did sometimes: instead of catching the Frisbee, he would jump over it.

I sent the e-mail before I could talk myself out of it and then I started picking at my hangnails because it wasn't every day that I sent a flirtatious e-mail to a girl I didn't know. Then I realized how stupid the e-mail was. How stupid it sounded. I re-read it. It was all wrong, wasn't it? It didn't strike the right note at all.

Then the phone rang. Frick.

But for some reason, I was ready. Sort of.

"This is Jack," I said.

"Hi, Jack. It's Callie. My dog says Flip is cute but looks like he's probably a spaz."

"She's right," I said.

"That's good," she said. "That's what she likes." Then she reminded me that in ninth grade, we had been in a play together. "The one about the chess competitors who fall in love," she said.

"Oh, yeah, *Check Mates.*"

"The one and only," she said.

"Who did you play?" I asked.

"I was Veronica Rutherford's chess coach."

"Oh, yeah," I said. I remembered Callie now. She was cute. She was funny.

She asked me if I wanted to take a drive up north, see the Field of Dreams in Dyersville—the actual cornfield baseball diamond where they shot the film. I said that'd be great. We arranged to meet in about an hour. She insisted on driving.

After I hung up, I furrowed my brow. "What just happened here?" I said out loud. Ten minutes ago I barely knew this girl; now we were going on a date in an hour. How had that transpired? Why hadn't she been offended by my horrible e-mail? What had happened to the old Jack Grammar, the one that would have flubbed it somehow?

Well, I reasoned: I could still flub it. Let the flubbing begin!

chapter 9

TO KEEP MYSELF OCCUPIED WHILE I waited, I unloaded the dishwasher. I vacuumed my room. I swept the front porch. I flattened some cardboard boxes for recycling. I put air in Mom's bicycle tires. I cleaned Flip's water bowl. And I cleaned all the mirrors in the house. And the mirrors in both cars. Actually, I was still cleaning the rearview mirror on the Camry when Callie drove up and honked. She was in a little orange Civic—one of the button-cute ones from the late '70s.

She got out and came over and I introduced myself and dropped the bottle of Windex on her toes.

"Oh, man, sorry," I said. She was wearing flip-flops and had very small toenails. They were painted white.

"Hold on," she said, "there's a delayed 'ow' coming." She held up a finger. Then after a bit she said, "Ow."

To make it up to her, I cleaned her car's mirrors and then buffed them.

"Little spot there," she said, pointing, and I touched up her side mirror. It felt good to have something to do because I didn't know what to say. She must have thought I was pretty cool, what with my bottle of Windex and all.

We drove north. She was one of those people at City High who took the same kind of classes I did and liked the same teachers and so forth but whose path had rarely crossed mine. It was a big school, after all. So we talked about school—I could talk with anyone about school—and the evening was bright and I felt myself relaxing. Callie was easy to talk to and she asked a lot of questions and she drove exactly the speed limit. I felt a little bit like we were on a field trip. Was that what dates were supposed to be like?

We got to Dyersville and walked out onto the Field of Dreams. There was a father pitching underhand lobs to his little daughter and when the daughter finally connected with a pitch, the ball blooped up and Callie made like she was going to catch it, but she fumbled it at the last second.

"You did that on purpose," I said after the girl had rounded the bases as if she'd hit a home run.

"I didn't want to get that poor girl out on her only hit," she said.

We walked the bases and wandered into the outfield and soon we had the field to ourselves and I said, "How do you feel about the actual movie *Field of Dreams*?"

"Oh, it's horrible," she said.

I sighed. "Thank God we agree on that."

"I mean, Kevin Costner?" she said. "Please."

"Tell me about it," I said, and for some reason it became more difficult to converse after that. Sunset was approaching, and the blue sky above us was darkening. A breeze was moving across the field now, and Callie crossed her arms. I was shy, and I looked at Callie and she was smiling even though we weren't talking, and she had this little gap between her front teeth. I liked that little gap.

We picked up some burgers on the way out of town and ate as we drove. At least that gave us something to do and the silence between us wasn't as embarrassing. But then while we ate, we started trading stories about our family pets over the years, and normally I would have been bored out of my gourd listening to someone's pet stories, but Callie's stories were so warm and so funny that by the time she was telling the story of the day that her cat Jessie Lee rode in the bed of the plumber's pickup truck all the way to Cedar Rapids, I was basically laughing nonstop.

We drove on through the countryside as the night gathered itself about us, and we rolled up the windows as it got cooler, and the colors in the west brooded and then darkened and then disappeared. We started assigning human professions and belongings to our pets—Flip, we decided, was a systems analyst who liked his Dockers and his Pottery Barn furniture. I liked the way Callie's key chain was jingling below the ignition, and the dashboard lights made her face glow and I felt happy.

But I also felt pretty lame because by the time we made it back to town, we were silent again, and I was thinking about what to say and how to act when we said good night. I mean, I didn't know how to move things forward. It was like I was missing some vital piece of chromosome that ruled such instincts. I was a genetic freak. Kind of like the X-Men, but with superlameness instead of a superpower.

"Jack," Callie said when she stopped in front of my house. "I really don't know what to say right now."

I nodded. I swallowed. Could she read my mind? "That's okay," I said. Here she was, saying the same thing that I was thinking. It just made me like her more, but it didn't help me talk smoothly. It had never occurred to me that there might be girls who were just as awkward and weird around the opposite sex as I was. Maybe I just had to find one of them and everything would be okay! Maybe Callie was that person.

"I know you're a lot cooler than me and everything," she said. "I mean, you're really with it and I think your dog is great and it doesn't even really bother me that you would have caught that girl's fly ball and gotten her out."

"I know," I said. I know? I know what?

"But anyway, I'm not good at saying stuff life this, so good night, and I hope maybe we can go to other places together and everything. Sometime. Again. You know."

"Yeah," I said. And I sat there, looking at the dashboard. I opened and closed the glove compartment—which was an extremely weird thing to do at that particular moment—and then I said good night and I tried to smile at her really broadly as I got out of the car, but I think she probably didn't see it in the darkness and as I walked away, I felt stupid and powerless and wistful.

I watched her drive off. "She's kind of like me," I said, and it made sense and I liked thinking about that. I felt tired from the date because of all the silences. But there was also a part of me that felt really connected to Callie and also connected to myself. She had been warm and funny and when she dropped that girl's fly ball, I knew exactly what she was doing.

I'd been standing in the darkness in front of our house for however many minutes, reliving the date, when I noticed a car sitting just up the street with its engine idling. Its headlights came on and it moved toward me. The window rolled down.

"Hey, Jack!" a girl screamed from inside. There were two girls— one driving, one in the passenger's side. "Look what we did!"

They turned on the cabin light and began howling, and they lifted their shirts and revealed their breasts. On each breast a letter was written crudely with a thick black marker. Their breasts spelled CKJA.

"Are you guys on the list?" I asked.

They were still howling. They were obviously drunk. I could smell it.

"Excuse me," I said.

"Jack! Jack! Jack!" they said.

"Pick us!" the driver said. "You can take both of us to the prom! We're a package!"

"I don't understand your breasts," I said. This was not the kind of sentence I thought I would ever say in my life.

They looked down at their chests.

"Oh," the passenger said. "Look!" she said to the driver, and she pointed to her chest. "We're backwards!" They burst out laughing.

"Wait—I get it now," I said.

"Let's switch places," the passenger said.

"Yeah!" the driver said.

I tried to discourage this, but to no effect, and after a great deal of screaming and wriggling the two girls finally switched places and redisplayed their chests. Now the letters made sense: JACK. I asked them their names. Yes, one of them was on the list. Her response to the ad had been very short and utterly without intelligence. I told them that it was nice to meet them but that unfortunately I wouldn't be able to go to the prom with them.

As I walked away, they kept yelling, "But we're a package! You get us both! A package!"

Inside the house almost all the lights were off. I took some cookies from the kitchen and went upstairs. I was too tired to think things through properly. I put my cookies down and slumped on my bed and tried to picture Callie Cunningham's face. I could almost do it, but not really, and this made me sad. What color were her eyes? I didn't know. I hadn't asked her enough questions, had I? I hadn't been very funny, had I? I hadn't even gotten her phone number, had I?

I felt emptied by the day. Two dates in one day. Okay, maybe it was more like one and a half dates in one day. Previous to today, I'd had two dates in two years, and now this. And I had how many dates to get through this week? Twenty more?

And the girls with their letter boobs? Did I really need that kind of provocation? No, I didn't. But if I was going to go through with 24/7, I would just have to put up with that kind of stuff. Besides, seeing breasts was never really a *bad* thing, was it? No.

In my e-mail in-box I found a surprise. A response from FancyPants:

Dear Jack,

You gotta believe. You just gotta believe, you know, that everything you need is already inside you and that all the cockamamie bullshit that you're dealing with is just a test of sorts. Prom doesn't mean anything, you know? It's fake, it's frilly, it's not real. It's a fabrication. It's an illusion. And if you expect it to change your life, you're deluded. But you can change your life yourself. You dig?

That's all I want to say.

Yours,

Miss FancyPants

It was like she was speaking directly to me at this precise moment. She knew exactly what I was going through, exactly what I was feeling. Suddenly I felt like the answer to everything— to prom, to my awkwardness—was *her*. FancyPants. If only I could meet her . . .

Who was she? I had to know. Maybe she was my soul mate, maybe we would go to the prom together and then never be separated for the rest of our lives. I sat staring at her words. She obviously knew a little about me. But it wasn't Natalie. She would have told me when I asked her about FancyPants. Plus this writing was more sophisticated than Natalie's. It couldn't be Pamela. That was just weird.

Was it Lucy, my running partner from the Firefly Club? But I hadn't even mentioned the prom to her, had I?

Was it some other girl on the list? Was it Callie?

It was maddening to not know who she was. If only I could meet her, unveil her, I could just end this 24/7 silliness and go to the prom with her. *She* was the prom magic that was going to happen to me, one way or another.

Suddenly my computer chimed, and an IM popped up. From FancyPants.

FANCYPANTS: jack grammar

Holy smokes. Here she was, online, as if I had summoned her simply by thinking about her.

JackFlash: FancyPants?
FANCYPANTS: i
FANCYPANTS: do
FANCYPANTS: you
FANCYPANTS: do
FANCYPANTS: too?
JackFlash: Hello?
FANCYPANTS: believing in
FANCYPANTS: or being believed in
FANCYPANTS: i do
FANCYPANTS: i do
FANCYPANTS: and
FANCYPANTS: i know so
FANCYPANTS: and
FANCYPANTS: i feel so
FANCYPANTS: and
FANCYPANTS: therefore
FANCYPANTS: it is real
FANCYPANTS: . . . .
FANCYPANTS: now
FANCYPANTS: and
FANCYPANTS: then
FANCYPANTS: (both)

I watched the messages come up, each accompanied by the chime of my computer, and I could picture her somewhere across town, typing. I could *feel* her words, but I didn't quite understand them. I *absorbed* them. She was communicating so directly with me—like no one ever had—that I was stunned by the power of it. I was off balance but riveted.

But what to say? She hadn't sent a message in at least a minute.

JackFlash: You know me?
FANCYPANTS: yes yes
JackFlash: Who are you?

No response.

JackFlash: Are you on the list?
FANCYPANTS: no no
JackFlash: Would you like to be?

She didn't respond. I sent the message again and waited, but nothing came back. She was still online, but . . .

I picked up my cell phone and dialed Natalie. Her line was busy. I left her a voice mail.

"WHO IS FANCYPANTS!" I said. "I want to know." I hung up.

FancyPants and I were online for another twenty minutes. I didn't write anything more to her—I was afraid of breaking the spell, of scaring her away. Plus I didn't know how to respond to her impassioned poetry. And she didn't write anything more to me. We just hung out without writing any more messages. Finally, she disappeared.

When I shut down the computer and stood up, my legs were numb from sitting cross-legged on my bed for so long. And my bare feet felt something prickly on the carpet. I looked down. Crumbs. Cookie crumbs. I'd put the cookies on the floor when I first turned on the computer half an hour ago. But I'd forgotten to eat them.

"Flip?" I said. His head popped up. He was curled up on his doggie beanbag. He gave me his guilty face. Or maybe it was his don't-blame-me-I'm-just-a-little-doggie face.

Anyway, that's how utterly engrossed I'd been while IMing FancyPants: I didn't even notice my own damn dog eating my own damn cookies.

chapter 10

I DIDN'T DREAM OF COOKIES. I dreamed of cake. A gigantic cake. It was round, had several layers, and was so big it was sitting in the middle of the football field—that was the only place that could hold it. And the top of the cake was covered with cherries—a big, goopy field of cherries.

I watched from the sidelines as Percy appeared on some kind of modified dirt bike. He did a wheelie in front of the crowd and they cheered and took pictures. The motorcycle had a huge knife sticking straight up from the gas tank—a six-foot-tall knife. In this way, the bike kind of looked like a shark with a very shiny and very tall top fin.

Percy himself was dressed in a sparkly jumpsuit and tall black boots. His helmet was black. He drove over to where I was sitting and I was worried he was going to ask me to get on. I was prepared to say no. But he merely did a donut on the turf near me and then sped toward the cake at breakneck speed. What the frick was he thinking? That cake wasn't the kind you could just drive a motorbike over! It was a giant cake, the kind of cake that songs are written about, the kind of cake that you could fall onto

from a great height without injuring yourself. A cake of monu-
mental proportions!

(Just think of the oven!)

Now: but onward he zoomed, engine whining, obviously aim-
ing right at the cake, and when he hit the thing, frosting flew, and
the people in the crowd reached for the globs of frosting shrapnel
as they shot through the air. Those who were lucky enough to get
some frosting ate it.

My eyes were on the dirt bike, though. It disappeared immediately into the dark innards of the giant cake, and the buzz of its
engine faded, and I wondered if it would ever appear again. But
then I realized what was happening. The knife atop the bike was
cutting through the cake, and I watched the tip of the knife—
barely visible—cross the wide expanse of glistening cherries. And
finally the knife reached the far side, the roar of the dirt bike
returned, and Percy and his bike exploded out of the cake.

He was cutting the cake into slices.

The process took several minutes—he had to make twelve
passes through the cake—and the crowd grew more and more
ecstatic. They loved it, even more than football. They were all
splattered with frosting by now, and when they weren't cheering, they were licking the frosting off their arms and collars and
neighbors.

And when it was done, when Percy finally shut down his
miraculous cake-knife motorbike, there were exactly twenty-four
pieces of huge cake, and I watched, paralyzed with fear, as teams
of girls poured onto the field, heaved the individual pieces onto
huge plates with wheels, and rolled them toward me.

Twenty-four pieces . . .

No! Not me! I'm not hungry. I'm full already! I'm full!

But the cake came closer and closer. And a giant fork was handed to me. A pitchfork-sized fork. And the cake came closer, closer, closer . . .

I was going to have to eat it all.

So, after that kind of dream, Monday morning was a welcome arrival. Percy picked me up as usual. I looked at him a little suspiciously.

"Hey," he said in greeting.

I nodded. We drove off. "Cake," I said quietly.

"What?" he said.

"I don't like cake," I said.

"Whatever," he said. "More for me."

Despite our friendship of ten years (we'd met in Cub Scouts when our two self-built cars were the only ones not to cross the finish line in the Pinewood Derby), Percy and I came from different worlds, and we were headed to different galaxies. He was a kid raised by his working-class grandparents, constantly pummeled by his older brothers, not particularly engaged by school. I, on the other hand, was raised by overeducated, sensitive parents, coddled by my sisters, and a solid A student. He was "thinking about" getting a two-year degree from the community college. I was headed east to college in three months. He had always had a way with girls; I'd only kissed two. He didn't care about being cool, yet somehow he always was; I wanted to be cool but hadn't been since fifth grade. And perhaps the biggest difference—what I'd realized recently—was that Percy wasn't afraid of anything. Me, I had spent high school scared of everything. Fear of failure. Fear of humiliation. Fear of bad breath. Fear of being laughed at. Fear of being different. Fear of not being happy. Fear of not being liked. Fear of not knowing who I was and what I wanted . . .

"Percy," I asked as we drove into the school parking lot, "how much do you like Penelope?"

This wasn't the kind of thing we usually talked about, and he gave me a strange look.

"You want to ask her to the prom?" he asked.

"No, I just . . . I just . . . It's just, how do you know that she's the one for you?"

He shrugged. We passed Seth Freelander on the sidewalk. Percy leaned out the window. "Hey, suck it, Freelander!" he called. Seth made a vulgar gesture. They were friends.

"Now, what was that you just asked?" Percy said to me.

"Nothing."

"Listen," he said, "you try things out. If it works, it works. If it feels right, it is."

"What if nothing ever feels right?" I asked. Nothing except being alone, I thought.

He stopped in a parking space and pulled the hand brake.

"This is a nice mother-daughter conversation we're having," he said.

He was right—this way of talking was ridiculous.

"Let's look at it this way," he said. "It's kind of like you've been living in a cave all your life, and now you've finally come outside and are blinded by the sun. But wait a little while and you'll get used to the sun. You'll even get a nice tan."

"Good metaphor," I said.

"I don't know what the heck a metaphor is, but thanks."

"I get what you're saying," I said. "That's all."

"Good. Oh, by the way, me and Penelope and you and Sarah Shay are going on a double date after school."

The mention of the word *date* made my ears ring. "What?!"

"You know Sarah. She's on the list now. It's cool, right?"

I willed myself to calm down. I inhaled. I exhaled. "Yeah," I said. "It's cool."

"We'll meet you here after school. And we're going to have a most thrilling double date, right? And there will be none of this touchy-feely crap from you, right?"

I pointed at him. "You're a bad friend," I said.

"Eh," he said, shrugging. "I can't please everybody. Dillweed."

As we walked toward the school, my cell phone rang.

"Hello?" I answered.

"Hi, Jack. It's Kaylee."

"Kaylee . . ." I said, drawing a blank for a moment. That was a nice moment, then I remembered who she was. She was kind of the queen bee of the fashion brigade. She was one of the people who fancied herself to be at the top of the school social pyramid, when in fact everyone knew it wasn't a pyramid at all; it was more of a puddle. "Oh, hey, Kaylee . . ."

"Yeah, hey," she said. "So I'm just wondering if you'd thought about things yet?"

"Uh, yeah, some," I said. Yes, she was one of the original people on the list. I remembered her response:

DANCINGQUEEN171717@hotmail.com
    Hey Jack, Kaylee Pritchett here. Everyone is saying that I'm a shoo-in for prom queen, but I think it would be totally embarrassing to go without a date. (You heard how Scott Brader broke his ankle sliding into home plate and will have to be in a wheelchair for two weeks? As if I'd go to the prom with someone in a wheelchair!) So that's why I'm writing to you. If you don't pick me,

whatever, that's your loss, but seriously don't tell anyone I wrote to you b/c if you do, I'll deny it and it's not like they'd believe you anyway. I'm not including a picture because I'm sure you know what I look like. Remember, I'll squash you like a bug if you say a word about this.

The picture she'd sent with the e-mail was of a fluffy white kitten—obviously not her own kitten, but the kind of picture that would be on a kitten calendar.

I looked around. "Where are you?"

"I'm across the parking lot."

"I don't see you."

"I'm in my Touareg, of course."

I looked around, then spotted the SUV. "Oh, I see you. Why don't I come over so we can talk face-to-face?"

"No!"

"Uh . . . okay."

"I don't really want to be seen with you until we have an agreement on the terms."

"Very flattering," I said.

"But don't you understand?" she said.

"Listen, Kaylee. Here's what I understand: there's no way I'm going to go to the prom with you."

I hung up. I *thought* that I heard a muffled scream of rage in the distance, as if someone was screaming inside their forty-thousand-dollar SUV.

"Who was that?" Percy asked.

"Kaylee Pritchett," I said.

"Give me that," he said, reaching for my phone.

"Why?"

He took it, went to my incoming call list, and pressed talk. I heard Kaylee answer.

"And another thing," he said, "I'm voting for Courtney Besser for prom queen, so stuff that in your glory hole!" He hung up.

"Thanks," I said. "Very helpful."

He handed me my phone. "My pleasure."

The phone rang.

"Don't answer that," he said. "She'll just yell at you."

I let it ring.

"Anyway," Percy said, "I'm very happy with your performance just now. We were hoping you'd dispose of Kaylee quickly."

"Why'd you even put her on the list?"

"Oh, you know, variety, selection. I know you like those clean-cut girls. Plus she bribed us."

chapter 11

THE REST OF THE MORNING went pretty well. Or at least it went better than it could have. This being the first day of school since the stupid prom ad appeared, I was afraid that everyone would be laughing and pointing at me. They did. Some.

In AP physics, for example, we split up into task groups and Stan Paprakeesh was trying to explain a simple probability formula to us and as an example he said, "Let's say someone places a personal ad online, a very awkward and ill-conceived personal ad, and they receive, oh, two responses, and of those responses . . ." And so on. At the end of which, I just asked him who *he* was going to the prom with, and he said he wasn't going to the prom because he didn't care to and Vanessa Jorgen laughed at him.

Also, someone wrote *Fondle my butt* on my locker with lipstick.

A few people asked me if I'd chosen my prom date yet, but they were nice about it. Most people seemed completely ignorant about the whole thing.

And Kaylee kept calling and leaving threatening messages on

my voice mail, so I had to turn my phone's ringer to silent. Actually, I felt good about having told her off. I kept thinking of what FancyPants had said in her e-mail last night—that prom couldn't change me, but that I could change myself—and I felt that turning down Kaylee was a small step in that direction.

In English, I scribbled in my notebook, trying to reconstruct the IMs FancyPants had sent me . . . *I feel so, I know so . . . Believing in, or being believed in . . .* It was mesmerizing, but I couldn't remember it all.

Between second and third period a girl came up to me at my locker. She was as tall as me and had dark hair and doe eyes and maybe just a bit too much makeup on. As she got close to me, she wobbled on her big purple platform shoes and had to put a hand against the lockers to keep from falling. It was very cute.

"Jack? I'm Samantha Milligan. I'm on the list."

"Oh, hi," I said, and not knowing what else to do, I stuck out my hand and she shook it. When she shook my hand, I could tell she was trembling. She was nervous. Her eyes were wide. I realized she was younger than me.

"I'm just wondering how everything's going," she said, "and I wanted to give you my phone number."

At that moment her messenger bag slipped off her shoulder and fell and a bunch of French flash cards spilled out. We both knelt and collected the cards without saying anything. She was blushing, and I felt bad for her but I didn't know how to put her at ease.

"What year are you, Samantha?" I asked.

"Freshman," she said. I handed the last of the flash cards back to her.

"I think there's been a mix-up," I said. "You have to be a junior or senior to get on the list." It was a lie, but the more I looked at her, the younger and more frightened she seemed. I couldn't go to the prom with someone more afraid of it than me. And I didn't want to scar the poor girl by rejecting her in the middle of the hall. I figured rejection by technicality would be kinder.

"Oh!" she said. "I'm sorry. I'm so, so, so sorry. I didn't know."

"It's no big deal," I said.

But as she walked away—still wobbling in her shoes—I had an idea. I had felt some kind of connection with her, so I called to her.

"Samantha," I said. She turned around and stood there in the middle of the hallway, looking lost.

"Come back," I said, motioning her over.

She walked over, and her eyebrows were arched. She thought I was going to change my mind or something.

"You're FancyPants," I said.

Her brow furrowed. She was confused. "No . . ." she said, "I'm Samantha Milligan. . . . I . . ."

"No, I understand," I said. "It's just that there's this girl who's been e-mailing me anonymously and I thought you might be her, maybe, and I just had to ask."

"Oh," she said. But she still looked confused, and I could see her eyes filling with tears. She thought that having already rejected her, I was now poking fun at her. I needed to explain myself better.

"I, uh, it's okay," I said. "This FancyPants person, I don't know who she is and I was just asking, just wondering. . . . It's a long story, but I don't . . ."

But it was no good, she was actually crying now, and the warning bell rang, and we had to rush to get to our classes.

So I ended up scarring her after all.

Percy, Penelope, Natalie, and I ate lunch outside, per my request. I told them I wanted to eat outside because of the weather—it was warm, sunny, and perfect—but really I just wanted a little bit of quiet in the middle of the day.

"I *swear,* Jack," Natalie said as she picked the tomatoes from her sandwich, "*I don't know who FancyPants is. Okay?*" Natalie was wearing her lovely red rain boots, which only she could pull off (literally and figuratively) and which she only wore on sunny days. "If I had a clue, I'd tell you. Although to be honest, she just sounds like a meddler. If she won't tell you who she is, then what's the point?"

"What are the rules for me dating people not on the list?" I asked.

Percy and Natalie looked at each other.

"That's awful adventurous, buddy," Percy said.

"As if you don't have enough on your plate?" Natalie said.

"Twenty-four girls isn't *that* many," Penelope said. "I must've dated, like, five times that many guys before I met Percy."

We all looked at Penelope for a moment.

"It's your life," Natalie said to me. "Date who you want."

"No," Percy said, "I say he has to stick to the list. I think that should be the rule."

"How about he gets one wild card?" Penelope said. "So, like, he can use the wild card to go on a date with one person who's not on the list."

They agreed to that, without my input.

"Why am I even agreeing to follow these rules?" I asked. "They're all made up."

"So is prom," Natalie said.

"Exactly," said Percy. "So ha."

Sarah Shay was one of Penelope's friends, and she was part of that whole bohemian-alternateen set that I had never been completely at ease with. Their shoes were just way cooler than anything I had ever owned. Not that I couldn't go out and steal a pair of bowling shoes from Colonial Lanes or buy some old hobo shoes at Goodwill, but why would I?

After school Percy drove us all out to the dam at Coralville Reservoir. We looked at the water rushing out of the bottom of the dam, then walked up the road. There was a fishy smell in the air, but it faded the farther we walked. Percy and Penelope were being lovey-dovey, which made me feel awkward, and Sarah was very quiet. We walked down into the fossil gorge. It was sort of a wide rocky wash off to the side of the dam.

After wandering for a while, I looked around and realized Percy and Penelope were gone. They were happily off on their own somewhere. So it was just me and Sarah.

"I don't know anything about the fossil gorge," I said. It was the best thing I could come up with.

"You don't?" she asked, and her face kind of lit up. "Really?"

"No," I said.

"I love the fossil gorge," she said. "I dream about the fossil gorge. Sometimes I think I *am* the fossil gorge."

Clearly I'd hit on something.

"Why?" I asked.

And she started waxing poetic about the wide, shallow seas that used to cover all of the Midwest millions of years ago. They were nutrient-rich seas, teeming with corals and crinoids and brachiopods. As the years passed, the water disappeared, and slowly soil accumulated and covered the old seabed and the prairie came and the buffalo roamed and Indians set fire to the tall grasses each year and the sky was wide and the nights were dark and the Iowa River meandered under the trees.

She paused for a long time, looking around at the evening, but she wasn't done.

And then, she explained, this dam was built in the middle of the last century and then in 1993 the flood of floods came and overwhelmed the dam so that water flowed over the emergency spillway—the first time that had ever happened. It was a raging river, pure white water, 17,000 cubic feet passing per second. ("That's 530 tons a second to you and me," Sarah said.) And all that roiling water scoured away fifteen feet of soil and four feet of limestone, and when the floodwaters receded, the ancient seafloor was revealed, rich with fossils from another time.

She gave me a tour of the gorge, showing me the best fossils, the undulating bedrock where the water had flowed long, long ago, and a mound of glacial-age soil that was left untouched by the flood because it sat in the wake of big rock. And then she showed me the holes where stones in the ancient Iowa River had vibrated in the current for hundreds of years and dug their own pits.

"They were trapped there," she said, "and all they could do was keep going down. So they did."

"That's funny," Percy said, suddenly behind us. "Because I feel like I go down all the time, too."

Penelope smacked him hard on the shoulder.

We stopped by the co-op for sandwiches—Sarah and I both choose the classic Cashew on a Hot Tin Roof—then ate them on the steps of the Old Capitol. Sarah was quiet again, and Percy and Penelope carried most of the conversation. But when they wandered off a little ways, Sarah said, "This is the only place in Iowa City you can come to see the sunset. Or at least the best place."

It was true, and I sometimes came here for exactly that reason, especially in the winter. The view encompassed not only much of the campus down in the river valley, but also the entire western horizon, which was dominated by the long and varied outline of the university hospital.

After dark we found ourselves wandering. We drove west across town, then east.

"I've got something at home that's pretty cool," Sarah said. So we headed there. And in the gloom of the backseat, I looked closely at her. She had black hair that hung very straight and shiny. Her neck was smooth and beautiful, and her eyes were slanted like a fox's. Even in the darkness I could see her freckles—beautiful constellations on her cheeks.

She lived out on Rochester Avenue, and she made us promise not to look as she loaded something into the back of Percy's station wagon. She then asked Percy to drive back to the river. So we came back down Rochester Avenue, passed the Drug Town pharmacy ("Drug Town!?" Percy exclaimed as we passed it. He always did that. "Drug Town!?"), cut through downtown on Market Street, and then crossed the river and parked by the big auditorium. From there we walked toward one of the long foot-bridges over the river. Sarah carried a big cardboard tube—about as thick as my leg—and I wondered what was inside it. She asked Percy and Penelope to wait at the end of the bridge. Then she and I walked to the center of the bridge. She taped the tube to the railing so that it was pointed straight up, and it finally occurred to me that there was nothing being carried in the tube—the tube itself was the thing we were there for. But what was it?

Then I saw the fuse.

She gave me a box of matches and asked me to light the fuse. We looked around. There was no one in sight.

I lit it.

"Now run!" she said, and took off toward Percy and Penelope.

We ran side by side, full tilt. I realized I'd been wrangled into something very illegal. We neared Percy and Penelope, and Sarah said we should all run farther, so we did. The four of us ran, then stopped on the shore of the river, a stone's throw from the bridge. For a moment I thought I could see the tiny glow of the fuse at the base of the tube, but then it blinked out.

Nothing happened.

"Jack lit it," Sarah said. I wasn't sure if this announcement was meant to cast blame on me if the thing didn't go off. Or maybe it was more of a legal pre-positioning in case we got caught and questioned by university security. Then again, it kinda sounded like she was proud of me—bragging.

"Is it a dud?" I asked.

"I think I can still see the fuse burning," Penelope said.

"I don't," I said.

"It is," Sarah said.

"This is going to be good," Percy said.

After another several seconds the wavering little glow of the fuse went dark for sure, and I was pretty certain that in fact the thing was a dud, but then there was a tremendous hollow *schwoooomp!* sound that was unlike anything I had ever heard. It seemed to suck the air out of my lungs. And there was a streak of something, some tiny spark jumping into the sky. But it disappeared immediately.

"Is that all?" Penelope asked.

"Just wait a second . . ." Sarah said.

We were all looking up now, but there was nothing to see. A college student passed us on the sidewalk and looked up to try to figure out what we were looking at.

"I think it's a dud," Percy said.

"Good," I said. I was breathing heavily from the sprint, and my hands were shaking, and Sarah was standing right beside me. We were touching.

"Wait for it . . ." Sarah said.

"It's been far too long," Percy said.

"One . . . more . . . second . . ." Sarah said.

"I'm sure it's dead by now," Percy said.

"Any . . . time . . . now . . ." Sarah said.

And then, at an altitude of what must have been thousands of feet, there was an explosion of great magnitude—but it was about a second before the firework's boom finally reached us. It was like the biggest sonic boom ever, and it echoed up and down the river valley. And meanwhile the firework's violet blossom was immense, covering a giant portion of the night sky. It was so bright the stars disappeared. The river in front of us lit up brilliantly, reflecting the firework like a mirror, so that I had the impression of being sandwiched between two still-expanding blasts, a kind of stereophonic bombardment.

That's when Sarah kissed me before I knew what was happening. Her mouth felt agreeably warm. And her eyelashes brushed my own.

Percy, still looking at the sky, said, "That can't be legal."

In the distance car alarms were going off.

Sarah and I ended our kiss and she suggested that we all run again, as fast as we could.

We did.

chapter 12

WE DROPPED SARAH OFF. Then Percy dropped me off at my house at about eleven. I stood in the backyard for a while, looking up at the stars. I thought about Sarah. I had known who she was for years, but really I didn't know her. And after tonight I felt like I had discovered a new and wonderful thing that had been right under my nose all this time. Her quietness seemed to arise from calmness. I liked that. And the calmness contained sparks—that was what was so great about it. Looking at the stars reminded me of her.

In my room, as I waited for my laptop to boot up, I remembered my cell phone. I'd turned it off this morning and forgotten to turn it back on. I checked my voice mail. In addition to twenty messages from Kaylee Pritchett, there was one from Natalie and one from Laura Gilden.

Laura Gilden! I remembered going trick-or-treating with her when we were both six or seven. We were with three or four other kids and Laura's mother ushered us around Iowa City, hitting only the richest neighborhoods. I was a Teenage Mutant

Ninja Turtle and Laura was a princess. Our haul of candy was enormous, and at the end of the night we all went back to Laura's house, which had a basement playroom about as big as a gymnasium. We spread out our candy on the carpet and started trading, and one by one everyone else left and then it was just me and Laura. And we continued trading, and I realized that I was slowly losing my candy horde. She was a wily trader. And at a certain point I agreed to accept kisses in exchange for candy. She would pick out two or three pieces of candy from my pile, then ask the price—which was always one kiss. She would kiss me softly on the cheek, take the candy, and then begin the process again. By the time I left her house, my plastic pumpkin was empty.

Now that we were in high school, I was still some kind of teenage mutant turtle (minus the ninja), hiding in my shell, and she was one of the princesses of the school, in full control of her social realm. She was beautiful and tall. And when she was nice to you, everything was good.

And she was now on the list. For a second I wondered: why the heck would Laura Gilden want to go to the prom with me? The best answer was: who cares?

I snuck out of the house and waited at the end of the block. She picked me up at exactly midnight. She drove a black Miata, and we crossed town with the top down and the music loud. The stars were shining above us, and the night was almost warm—the first night of the year you didn't need a jacket. We talked about grade school—about Mrs. Mead and her amazing wardrobe of sweaters that were somewhere between red and orange; about

Dylan Frisco, who sat on a pencil and cried in despair because we all knew that pencil lead is what gave you lead poisoning; about the time three pet rats got loose in the lunchroom. Mainly we laughed. I liked that even though Laura was one of the cooler girls in school, she still thought a lot about things that happened back then—a time when, we both agreed, things were just better all around.

We parked in the empty lot of the country club, under the darkness of the trees. I expressed my concern about being here after the club had closed for the night, but she said not to worry, that there would be no problem, and she kissed me on the cheek and that's all it took. I would follow her anywhere.

We walked to the back of the club, across the dewy grass, and came to the chain-link fence beside the pool. The water of the pool was black and glassy in the night, and I heard the pump in the distance. Before I knew it—and without my help—Laura boosted herself over the fence and told me to do the same. I voiced my concern about the possibility of getting caught trespassing, and she said nonsense, this wasn't trespassing, her father was one of the most important members of the club, and in fact if she had wanted to, she could have actually brought his keys and let us in by the front door. But I just stood there. Sneaking out was one thing. Breaking and entering was another. I was Jack Grammar. I didn't do things like this.

I looked at her through the fence. She was one of the few girls in school with a really short haircut; I liked that she was confident enough not to need a curtain of hair to hide behind. And she had this magnificent Roman nose. Other girls made fun of it sometimes, but to me it was absolutely perfect.

She motioned me over.

"What?" I whispered.

"Put your cheek there," she said, "against the fence."

After a moment I did. I could tell what was coming.

She kissed me on the cheek again—through the chain link—and the next thing I knew, I was scrambling up the fence. I did it with less grace than Laura, but I made it.

It was all like a dream.

We took off our shoes and walked across the smooth concrete. Laura asked me to sit down and she disappeared in the direction of the clubhouse. Soon she reappeared with a bottle and two glasses. What, they didn't lock doors around here? She sat down on the lounge chair across from me—our knees almost touching—and poured us two small drinks.

"I don't know . . ." I said, holding the glass in my trembling hands. "I—"

But before I could explain my reluctance, she kissed me again. So this was the way it was going to be. This was the pattern. Once again she was using kisses as trading trinkets.

"I remember, Jack," she said. "I took all your candy. All of it."

When she said that, I felt different. I felt like perhaps I *could* be a different person, a better person. I couldn't change the past, but I could determine my future. She downed her drink and looked right at me. I sniffed mine. I didn't even know what it was. There was about an ounce of liquid in the bottom of the glass.

I drank. It was like drinking heat or sun or fire. It burned its way into my chest, and at first it was an uncomfortable burn, but then it was a wonderful burn, a loving burn, a smoldering burn.

"See," she said. "No harm done."

I nodded.

"You are Jack Grammar," she said. "And this night is yours. And you should never let anything stop you."

I got goose bumps. I shivered. She refilled my glass and I looked at it and swirled the liquid and suddenly she was sitting right next to me on the concrete and she turned my head and kissed me on the mouth this time. Briefly. Softly. Warmly.

I lost count of how many times she refilled my glass. We sat hip to hip, and we looked out at the calm pool and the lights of Coralville strung out in the distance.

"Will you swim?" she asked me after a while.

"Swim?" I said. "Swim, swim, swim . . ." The word was a good one. The alcohol was changing me.

"Swim. Just swim," she said.

I leaned over. She kissed me on the mouth again. She tasted like whatever we were drinking.

"Okay," I said.

By the time we were standing at the edge of the water—she in her bathing suit, me in my shorts—I knew I was drunk. I couldn't feel my teeth. My face was hot. I couldn't quite tell where my skin ended and the night began. And most significantly of all, I wasn't nervous. I was collected. I was still inside, just like the pool in front of me.

And now, with my toes curled over the edge of the pool, I said, "One more."

"Okay," she said, smiling, and she kissed me yet again. I experienced the kiss as if it was something I was remembering instead of something I was actually doing. It seemed far away. Pleasant but not perfect. A bit awkward, perhaps, due to my lack of experience, but not embarrassing. Then I heard a splash, and I realized that the kiss was over, and Laura was in the water.

I went in, too.

Much later, I wrote to FancyPants. I spilled out the details of my day. I told the story of Kaylee Pritchett. I told her about traumatizing Samantha Milligan. I told her about both of the dates—the fossil gorge and highly illegal firework with Sarah, the drunk swimming with Laura. I lost track of everything I told her, I told her so much. It all seemed to come out. It kept going:

> I almost don't know where I am anymore. I almost don't recognize me right now. I remember the water and the stars and Laura Gilden. Her hair was wet. We floated. In the water. We floated. We laughed. A jet blinked in the sky and we watched it.
>
> It's late, isn't it? It's very late.
>
> The firework went up. We thought it was gone. We thought it was a dud. But it wasn't. It was huge. It was purple and bright.
>
> Everything is smooshed together. Everything is compressed right now. I feel like today was ten days long. I feel like the past three days have been a month so far. I look at what I'm doing—going out with these girls—and I don't see myself in the picture. Does that make sense? No, I guess not. I mean, everything has happened so fast that I haven't even had time to realize what's going on. What is going on?
>
> And what's the deal with all this kissing? Why can't I do it? Did I miss the day at school where they taught us? Can kissing be taught? I didn't do it right, I know. When Sarah Shay kissed me, our teeth crashed. When Laura Gilden kissed me, I think she laughed a little during it. I'm almost positive she did. And I would

never have had the guts to kiss Sarah. She had to do it herself. And I would never have kissed Laura if I hadn't been drunk.

Which I kinda still am. But for some reason, I can write very clearly, can't I? I can think very clearly.

I don't know, FancyPants. I don't know.

Who are you? I want to meet you. I want to know you. I want you to be my wild card. Do you hear me? I WANT YOU TO BE MY WILD CARD.

chapter 13

PERCY WAS GENERALLY NOT THE first person I wanted to see when I woke up. His choppy haircut. His massive cowlick. His sneer. His T-shirts with menacing slogans. Visually, he didn't provide for a pleasing transition from dreamland to waking.

"Bud, bud, buddy," he said, poking me.

My eyes opened. I thought I heard them creak like rusty hinges.

"Buddy boy," he said, poking me some more. "We're on a schedule here."

"No," I said. It was the only word I could think of.

"Really, we are," he said. He tapped his watch. "We've got fifteen minutes."

"Uh," I said.

"You slept through your alarm. Your parents are already gone."

I vaguely remembered Dad knocking on my door earlier. But my parents had learned long ago that their son was always reliable and that they didn't need to pull me out of bed themselves.

"You look terrible," Percy said. "And you smell funky. What the heck did you do last night?"

Speeding in Percy's rusty Toyota wagon toward school:

"Laura Gilden!" he shouted. "*Schweet!*"

"Enough shouting," I said, head in my hands. I didn't like being in the car—everything was moving too fast.

"How much did you drink?"

"I don't know," I said. I closed my eyes, but I could still *feel* the nauseating movement of the car. The hole in the muffler was approximately forty times louder than it needed to be.

"That much?"

"Yes, that much. I don't even know what we were drinking."

I looked at what I was wearing. Sandals? With socks? And jeans? Was I European all of a sudden? Percy had just thrown some clothes at me before we'd rushed out the back door. And I wasn't sure I had all my books with me. I wasn't even sure I had a frickin' pen.

My phone started ringing. It was the worst sound I'd ever heard. I sat on it. It stopped ringing.

"I feel unwell," I said.

"I can see that."

"Why didn't you tell me never to drink?"

"I think I did," Percy said.

I opened my phone and checked my voice mail. Who had just called?

"Yeah, hey, Jack. This is Scott Brader. Yeah, I just wanted to, you know, have a *chat* with you, head to head. I think you know why. So call me back, otherwise I'll corner you at school."

I shivered involuntarily. I blinked. Something sloshed around inside my stomach. Scott Brader? A *chat* with Scott Brader? He was Kaylee Pritchett's perennial boyfriend, the one who was wheelchair-bound with a broken ankle. His tone of voice in the message was scary—low and almost monotone. Clearly he was simply calling to arrange a time to pummel me to death. Head to head? Wasn't that just code for a battle to the bloody end? The harassing phone calls from Kaylee had stopped, but now she'd turned her boyfriend out on me.

Once, in the grade-school lunchroom, Scott had thrown a fork at me when I made a highly successful joke about his name (*Snot* Brader), and the fork stuck in my hair in a way that made it look like it was stuck in my head. It scared me so much that I ran to a teacher, crying—pretty sure that my brains were dripping out of my head—and clung to her legs like she was my mom. Scott got in trouble, and in retribution he pushed me off the jungle gym a week later. It was really the only violent run-in I'd ever had with anyone other than my sisters, and I still did my best to keep out of throwing range of Scott.

I knew one thing: there was no way I was going to call him back. He'd have to corner me at school, just like he threatened to. I wasn't going to make this easy for him. At least that way there would be witnesses to my demise.

"Was that Natalie?" Percy asked.

"Nobody," I said. I suddenly felt cold.

"Let's get back to our story," Percy said. "Tell me, how would you describe the nature of your biological interaction with Laura Gilden last night?"

"I wouldn't," I said. Everything about last night was just a blur to me, really. I had loved the attention Laura gave me, but I couldn't even remember much of what we'd talked about. It was like a date that didn't really happen, even though my hangover was proof of it.

"Aw, come on, you can tell Perc."

"No," I said.

"Are you saying you guys went night swimming without any exchange of bodily fluids?"

"We kissed, okay? I don't want to talk about it." My stomach was in some horrible kind of spin cycle.

"Why not? What's the story? Isn't this what you wanted? Isn't this the whole point? I mean, you kissed two girls in one night! So what's the problem?"

I said, "I think I'm going to be sick."

Percy smiled. "My baby's first hangover . . ." he said. "It's cute."

Luckily the window was open. I leaned out just in time.

I felt better after that, but not much. My stomach was rebellious. I had a dull and heavy headache that made me wish for the quiet of a tomb. My eyes were dry; my mouth was cottony. My eyes were bloodshot and they stung and Mrs. Cicero, just passing me in the hall, said that one of them seemed to be larger than the other. Plus my mind was not operational. I sat in calculus and tried to pay attention. Mr. Franconi was having one of his days where he was writing frantically on the board—talking all the while—and continually running out of space on the blackboard and having to look around for something to erase. Whenever he did this, he asked us for our input. "What can we erase here?" he'd ask. "What can we put to sleep?" he'd say. Then he'd find some diagram or formula and point it out and say, "Are we done with this one, people? Can we please put it to sleep?"

Can we please put *me* to sleep? I thought.

When the bell rang, I got up. The only way I was going to make it through the day was one footstep at a time. Someone tapped me on the shoulder. It was Adrian Swift, my locker neighbor, whom I'd spent so much time trying to avoid. Okay, fair enough. Bring it on, world. I was too weak to run or make extremely awkward excuses.

To top it off, she was on my list, as of yesterday.

"Hi, Jack," she said. "I've been meaning to talk to you."

I didn't even try to smile. I touched the bump on my head where I'd hit her locker door Friday.

"The thing is," I said to her, "I'm going to the prom with someone else. So that's that." Apparently I *was* up for making lame excuses. Score one for Jack Grammar!

"Oh," she said.

"That's the way the cookie crumbles," I said. And I stood there for a second, waiting for her to say something mean or ask me how my rickets were or something. But she didn't.

"I understand," she said simply. "I hope you have a good time."

Then she left.

I felt worse than I had all day. I didn't like lying, especially to someone as nice and modest as Adrian.

In addition, I was now nauseated and hungry at the same time.

I had agreed yesterday, via e-mail, to have lunch with Celia Proctor. I didn't know her at all, but I had seen her in a couple of the school plays and she was definitely a great actress. I didn't really want to have a schoolhouse lunch date with a drama queen, but nothing I did seemed to make me feel any better or any worse, so I figured I might as well go ahead with it. If I was lucky, I would at least keep my lunch down.

Celia was a bit taller than me, but I liked it. Maybe the way to say it is that she was long boned. She had a round-shouldered, slumpy posture, but there was something honest and endearing about it. She had long brown hair in a ponytail, and she was wearing baggy jeans and what appeared to be a cycling jersey. I wondered, briefly, if it was a costume for a play she was rehearsing.

We sat by ourselves out by the tennis courts and as soon as I asked her one question about what play she was working on, it was like the floodgates opened. She went on and on. Her eyes focused on the air in front of her and she made dramatic gestures as she talked.

". . . and so I thought that if instead of thinking about *conventional* blocking and lighting on a flat stage, if we actually built a set that consisted of several ascending 'levels'—like giant stairs— I could help emphasize the text's concept of hierarchy and classism, especially as it related to *my* character. I didn't want to play it too directly, so then I asked myself how I could really bring myself *out* of *acting*—you know, *away* from *performance*—and present myself to the audience in a fresh way. I knew I could do it. I knew I had gotten close to doing something like that when I was in *Halligan* last year, and I— Did you see *Halligan*?"

"Yes," I said. "My favorite part was—"

"Well, then you know how I was portraying Cynthia Devereau as more of a layered *caricature* than a character per se—which was my idea—I got it from watching old silent movies—and anyway, I started working on how I could 'project' myself without bringing attention to my *physical* form, and so I thought maybe I could—"

"Not bringing attention to your physical form?" I asked. All her talk was making me feel sicker than before.

"Yes, what I mean is—well, did you see me in *Direwood Landing* last fall at the Riverside Theatre—you know, the professional theater, not that community crap and not the school stuff?"

I had heard her question, but somehow I was just stunned. I couldn't answer because I could see that whatever I said would just bring on more talk about *her,* and *her* ideas, and *her* performances, et cetera.

"Yeah, I saw it," I said, "and I liked that part where the manta ray started singing."

"Well, then you know how in that play I had to portray twins in a way that didn't . . . that didn't . . ." She trailed off. She put her sandwich down. "Manta ray?" she said.

"Uh-huh," I said.

"What are you talking about?"

"The singing manta ray," I said.

"There was no singing manta ray in *Direwood Landing.*"

"I know," I said. "But I wish there had been."

"Are you *trying* to be annoying?" she asked.

"Ha!" I said. "That's hilarious, coming from someone who just spent eleven minutes in a monologue about themselves and their great ideas and their brilliant portrayals of incestuous twins!"

"What! I can't believe this. You asked me about my plays— you know that's what I *do,* that's who I *am*—and now you're complaining that—"

"Eleven minutes!" I said, tapping my watch. "I started timing you because I had a feeling this was going to happen."

She stood up and grabbed her backpack. "I can't believe I got talked into this," she muttered. "I'm sorry about your situation and everything, and I know I'm not supposed to mention that, but I don't care. It apparently doesn't excuse you from being a jerk."

"What?"

"You don't want women to succeed. You hate to see a successful woman. You think women should just be cheerleaders for whatever stupid things you're doing, which the last time I checked isn't much!"

She walked toward the school.

"You're wearing a cycling jersey!" I yelled.

Then I put down my apple and curled up on my side and suddenly there was a clap of thunder immediately overhead and it started raining. Raining hard.

It was hard to move. I lay in the rain and then I heard screams and people running down the sidewalk—splashing—rushing to get inside. I felt self-conscious and I got up and went back inside, too. I threw away the remnants of my meal and stood dripping inside the doors. There was another round of thunder and the rain got heavier. I was shivering.

What had just happened? We clearly hadn't clicked. But what was that stuff she said about being sorry about my "situation"? I didn't understand that. Why did she say she wasn't supposed to mention that? It didn't make any sense.

Well, what did I care? As long as I didn't have to speak with her (or more accurately, be spoken *to*) ever again.

chapter **14**

THE TOWN WAS QUIET after the storm. Tree limbs were down here and there. The air was muggy and warm, but in a comfortable way, and after getting home from school, I just lay on the couch in the parlor—which we called the funeral room because it was so quiet. Then I did a little reading, trying to keep up with some of the schoolwork that I'd neglected because of all the dating. Then I decided to go for a run.

I turned around after two blocks. My stomach and head weren't ready for running yet.

I ate a banana, threw the tennis ball for Flip for ten minutes, then went back upstairs and checked my e-mail. I had two e-mails from new girls on the list. I replied to them both and told them that I'd already decided to go to the prom with someone else, thanks anyway. After first using this excuse on Adrian Swift this morning, I found it to be an easy one to give. It wasn't a rejection, really, just a matter of fact. (Or in my case, fiction.) This way I wasn't the bad guy. I wasn't in the mood to go on any dates or think about dates or any of that stuff, so I just rejected them outright.

I got involved in a series of games of hearts online, and all the other players loved me because I was easy to dump the queen of spades onto. My mind still wasn't working, and I just couldn't play as well as usual, but I didn't care.

I quit playing and started writing an e-mail to FancyPants. She was the only person I wanted to talk to. She hadn't responded to my drunk e-mail yet from last night but that didn't stop me.

I didn't really know what to say in the e-mail, so I found myself struggling to write much.

That was a pretty cool storm, wasn't it? A lot of thunder, a lot of rain. I'm glad it's storm season again.

Didn't feel so good today. Maybe you could have guessed that.

Had a horrible date with someone at lunch. She just talked about herself and did a lot of air quotes and hand gestures. Very annoying. We got into a spat and she told me that she got talked into going out with me. And then she said, "I'm sorry about your situation and everything, and I know I'm not supposed to mention that." Isn't that bizarre? I can't figure it out. What situation is she talking about? Me having to go through this whole thing just to get a prom date? But why would she say she's not supposed to mention that?

Anyway . . . I'm feeling a little better now. How are you?

Jack

I sent the e-mail and then I felt pretty low about it because it was such a stupid e-mail. Her e-mails and IMs had been so fabulous, but here I was, just being the same old boring and lame Jack Grammar. It all was so annoying my head started to itch. I was bound to scare FancyPants away.

But suddenly FancyPants IMed me. I looked at the screen, kind of amazed. I hadn't known she was online.

FANCYPANTS: what was her name?

I blanked out. What was she asking?

JackFlash: Who?
FANCYPANTS: the girl u had lunch w/
JackFlash: Oh. Celia Proctor. Do you know her?
FANCYPANTS: no. just wondering.
JackFlash: Oh.

I waited. Nothing. I got nervous.

JackFlash: Cool.

That was the best I could do?

FANCYPANTS: don't worry. she's just 1 girl. sounds like u had good dates yesterday.
JackFlash: I guess.
FANCYPANTS: listen, i've been thinking about your kissing issues. what u have to do is tell a friend. someone w/ experience. someone u can trust.
JackFlash: But the more people I tell, the more real it becomes, the more embarrassing it is.
FANCYPANTS: i think it's the only way.
JackFlash: You're right. You're so smart. You're right. I'm going to call my friend Natalie right now.
FANCYPANTS: that sounds like a good plan. bye, jack.

But I had to do better than this. I *had* to.

JackFlash: So what do you say about being my wild card?
FANCYPANTS: you don't know who i am.
JackFlash: So tell me.

Nothing.

JackFlash: You're the only person I can talk to these days. I want to meet you.

Suddenly she was gone.

Apparently I'd scared her off. I shook my head. I was disappointed not only because she'd not been interested in meeting me, but because her role in the conversation had been big sisterly—giving me advice. Where was the poetry of Sunday night? Still, her advice was good. I picked up my cell and dialed Natalie, but then I panicked. What was I doing? Was I really going to spill my guts to Natalie about not being able to kiss? What was she going to do? Wave her magic wand? I hung up.

I called Percy instead. A little diversion was what I needed. A night without dates, without girls.

"'Lo?" he answered. Usually Mrs. Kowalski answered.

"Percy, it's Jack."

"Hey, buddy. What's the scoop?"

"No scoop here. Hey, you wanna bowl a game or two? Just us guys?"

"It's been a while since we did that, eh?" he said. "But I gotta stay here. Papa's in bed sick, and I should stick around. I promised him a game of dominoes."

"Oh. He okay?" Papa was his grandfather. He was actually one of the custodians at school. You know how every school has one old-timer janitor that everyone loves? That was Mr. Kowalski. He'd worked at the school since the 1950s.

"He'll be fine," Percy said. "He'll whup me at dominoes, as usual. He won't let me use a calculator."

There was some commotion in the background. It sounded like Percy's grandmother.

"What's that?" I asked.

"Ah, Grandma's been cooking all night, trying to get him to eat. And now she's yelling at him because he won't eat." Mr. Kowalski was one of the tiniest men I'd ever met, but he could eat like three or four normal-sized men. "And you know my grandmother: the more food piles up here, the more nervous she gets, so I'm eating all I can."

"Lucky," I said.

"Yeah, well . . ." Percy said. "So, take it easy. I'll catch you tomorrow."

After I said good-bye, I sat there, glum. I felt bad for Percy. Not because he had to stay in—he loved his grandparents and he always helped them out without complaint—but because his grandfather was sick. Here I was, worrying about prom and kissing and Percy was out there dealing with real life. As usual.

I dialed Natalie's home line again, ready this time to leave a message—just a breezy hello, give me a call. But Bridget picked up.

"Hey, Bridget!" I said. I was happy to hear her voice. "Short time, no see."

"Howdy, Jack."

"Is Natalie there?"

"She's out with Dan."

"Dan the man," I said, which was how almost everyone referred to him. "Well, I'll catch her later, then," I said.

"Hey," Bridget said, "you wanna go get ice cream?"

The drive west, into the apocalyptic, post-storm sunset, was the first refreshing and restorative thing I had done all day. Bridget sat in the passenger's seat, scanning for a radio station. She settled on a noxious pop station that was playing a teenybopper hit. I glanced over at her, and she was mouthing the words to the song. I was reminded how young she was.

Out in the countryside the bare fields were black—wet with the afternoon's rain. And in some fields, tiny corn sprouts looked like stitches on a dark quilt, running in straight lines across the hills.

On the phone Bridget and I had agreed that we didn't much care for Dairy Queen's soft serve, so we'd decided to head out to Jon's Ice-Cream Store in Tiffin, about fifteen minutes from home. When we got there and tasted our cones, we both agreed that this was better than DQ. More flavorful. More melty smooth. And the chocolate ice cream actually tasted like chocolate, not like dust.

"Hey," Bridget said, licking her twist cone.

"Hey, what," I said.

"Why don't we go on a search for the best soft-serve in the area?"

"Right now?"

"No, it would be an ongoing quest," she said. "I think it's a fitting quest, with summer coming. It's a presummer quest."

"Let's do it," I said. And we shook on it. Then it was back to the licking.

When we were done, we sat there with our tiny wadded napkins and we didn't feel like leaving yet. We were thirsty, so I got us two tiny cups of water. We watched the occasional car or pickup roll past.

"You seem tired," Bridget said.

"I am. But I feel better now."

I told her that I'd been out late, that this whole 24/7 schedule was killing me.

"It sounds a bit crazy," she said.

"What do you expect?" I asked. "It was Percy and Natalie's doing."

"Good point."

"It's wearing me out."

"You know, you could just hang out with me. You don't have to go to the prom. We could watch *The Goonies*. Do a soft-serve run. Play pinball."

"That's pretty much the best offer I've had," I said. "And I hope you're not surprised when I show up at your door Saturday night in my tux."

"That's the beauty of it," she said. "You wouldn't even have to wear your tux if you didn't want to."

"But I *could,* couldn't I?"

"Yes."

"Excellent."

Just as I dropped Bridget at her mom's house, Natalie drove up with Dan the man in his Cavalier.

"Hey!" Natalie yelled at me, jumping out of Dan's car. "Leave my little sister alone!"

"She's the one that asked me out," I said. "I'm the victim here."

"You think I believe that for one second?" Natalie said. "For *one second?*"

Then the joke was over. Bridget rolled her eyes. Dan got out of the car and waved at me. He was only about eight feet away, but he waved anyway. I waved back.

Natalie was looking at Bridget. She narrowed her eyes.

"Hey, that's my jacket," she said.

Bridget shrugged.

"You're supposed to *ask* before borrowing things," she said.

"Sure, *boss,*" Bridget said, and then went inside.

Natalie rolled her eyes.

"Hi, Dan," I said.

"Look at this watch," he said, and he held out his arm.

"Wow," I said. It was a huge watch with a huge watchband. It looked sort of like a speedometer that had been ripped from the dashboard of an old car.

"We just bought it," Natalie said. "He's *very* proud of it."

"I think it's fly," Dan said, admiring it. He said "fly" a lot, even though nobody else did anymore. Come to think if it, nobody had ever said "fly," really.

"That's the biggest watch I've ever seen," I said.

"Exactly!" he said, grinning.

"This is riveting," Natalie said.

"So how's the datefest going?" Dan asked me.

"Up and down."

"I heard you went out with Laura Gilden."

"Yeah."

"You're one impressive fellow," he said. "You're my idol."

"It's thanks to Natalie, really."

He squeezed her. "She's my all-time favorite idol."

"Aw, shucks," Natalie said, smiling broadly.

He and Natalie said good night. As always, they were very sweet with each other and it was a little embarrassing to watch. Then as he got in his car, he said, "Catch you later, Jackie. And be nice to the ladies."

Natalie and I went to her room and she relaxed and we talked and I found myself telling her everything about yesterday and today. About the mangled kisses. The hangover. The Celia Proctor incident. We laughed at that and about the weird stuff she said about people working hard just to get me a date. It was pretty funny, really, and Natalie said it just was further evidence that Celia tried to make drama where none existed.

"Now, kissing," she said, changing the subject. "What are we going to do about that?"

She asked me a lot of questions about the details of my kissing experiences and what techniques I'd used, and she gave me some pointers, but it didn't really make much sense to me. It was too abstract. It was like trying to teach someone how to ride a bike over the phone.

"Surely there's a better way to learn how to kiss," I said, exasperated.

"Not really," she said. "That's what junior high is for."

"I knew it! I knew I missed the class at some point. I took that damn band class instead of kissing class."

"Well, there is one thing," she said.

"What."

"Hm." She scratched her neck. "Hm, it's sorta weird. You have to promise me not to freak out."

"Okay," I said.

"Promise to remain calm."

"I promise. Does it involve fish?"

"No."

"Puppets? Do I have to kiss puppets?"

"No! I'm being serious."

"Okay, what?"

"We could kiss," she said.

"Huh?" I said. It didn't register. "We could kiss what?" I asked.

"*We* could kiss," she repeated. "*Each other.*"

"Oh."

"You and I. Me and you."

"Oh!"

"Us."

We looked at each other.

"I don't know," I said.

"Yeah, well, I mean, I'm just thinking out loud," she said.

I nodded. I shrugged. Then Natalie shrugged. She smiled nervously. It wasn't like her to smile nervously. She shook her head. I bent down from my seat on her bed and tightened my shoelaces. I felt uncomfortable.

Natalie said, "Well . . ."

Then we just burst out laughing.

"Me and you kissing?" I finally said. We kept laughing.

"I don't know what I was thinking!" Natalie said.

"I can't even picture it," I said.

Our laughing trailed off. We sat there. But talking about kissing had just made me more nervous than before, and I felt like I wanted to be alone, so I left.

chapter 15

"**BUT WOULDN'T IT JUST BE** weird?" I asked. I was back at home, and Natalie and I were on the phone. I'd left her house only fifteen minutes ago.

"I don't know," she said. "It's not the kind of thing I've done before."

"But—but . . ." I stammered. It was confusing.

"Okay," she said, "look at it this way. I've kissed a lot of guys, nearly all of whom I didn't know as well as I know you."

"True."

"And nearly all of whom I didn't like as much as I like you."

"Right."

"And nearly all of whom weren't really nice at all."

"Go on."

"But don't you see what I'm getting at?" she asked.

"Sort of."

"Why *shouldn't* we kiss?" she said. "Where is that written? What rule would we be breaking?"

"But what about Dan?" I asked. "I mean, I don't think he'd be a fan of this."

"I'm not proposing marriage," Natalie said. "It would all be for instructional purposes only. Dan won't mind. I won't even tell Dan anyway since that would be betraying your confidence."

"Yeah . . ." I said.

"It's all very much like that time you taught me to play backgammon."

"Kind of . . ." I said. Except backgammon is boring and it's a game and there's no physical contact. "Sort of . . ."

"I'm just talking out loud here. I'm just thinking about you. So . . ." she said. "I don't know. Why not? That's what it comes down to. Why not? You need help, and I can help you. That's what friends do. So why not?"

"Because it's weird," I said.

"So is life," she countered.

"Could I feel you up?" I asked.

She laughed. "No."

"I'm feeling very strange after that joke," I admitted.

"It'd just be like me helping you with homework or something. This is your homework: to learn how to kiss."

"I guess so."

"And it's not like anyone else in the entire world would ever have to know. Why would we ever tell anyone else?"

"Good point."

"So think about it," she said. "That's all I'm saying. I didn't mean to weird you out."

"Okay," I said.

"Good. Just think about it."

"No, I mean, okay, let's do it," I said.

"Really?"

"Yes. I think so."

"When?" she asked.

When? Immediately. I was on a tight schedule this week and the sooner this happened, the better. It was already nine thirty, so we had to do it now if we wanted to do it tonight.

Where? My room. Natalie was adamant about this, partly because she didn't want Bridget nosing around while we were "working" and partly because she said it should be in a private place where I was comfortable. My parents wouldn't think twice about me and Natalie being alone in my room.

While I waited for her to arrive, I paced. Then I tidied up my room a little. Flip followed at my heels. He knew something was brewing. I put all my CDs back into their cases. I put my dirty clothes into the hamper. I closed the closet door. I smelled my T-shirt, then put on a clean one. I went down the hall to the bathroom and combed my hair. I smiled at myself in the mirror, then decided to brush my teeth. It was the courteous thing to do. Then I smoothed my eyebrows. Then I washed my hands.

I sat at my desk and tried to read, but I could absorb nothing. I ended up reading the same paragraph over and over again.

When she tapped on my door, I snapped my head up, startled. She came in and we said hello and she took off her jacket and I saw that she'd changed her clothes, too. She had on black jeans and a short-sleeve button-down shirt. It was a very simple look for her. Normally she was a bit flashy, a bit colorful or racy. But here she was looking down-to-earth and sisterly. She even had on old running shoes. I'd never seen her wear running shoes except while playing sports, which she only did about twice a year.

Perkins County Schools
Media Center

"So . . ." she said. She sat on the edge of my bed.

I went over and closed the door, then I went and sat beside her. Flip was sitting in the middle of the floor, staring inquisitively at both of us. "Little doggie," I said. And I did a nervous laugh. I got up and opened the door and asked Flip to leave. He didn't move. Normally he obeyed immediately. He only left after I asked him a third time, then I closed the door.

"I don't know what to do with my hands," I said a few minutes later.

"That's something that will come naturally," Natalie said. "But for right now, put one here"—she moved one of my hands to her hip—"and one here"—and she put the other hand on her back, between her shoulder blades. This position brought our faces very close together. Her cheeks looked pinker than usual. But I couldn't tell if she was blushing or just wearing makeup.

"Now try again," she said.

I leaned in, closing the few inches between us, and brought my lips against hers. It was a static and off-target kiss.

"Wait," she said, pulling back. "Remember, kissing is not about *pressing*."

"Was I pressing?"

We kissed again.

"Or teeth," she said. "It's not about teeth, either."

"See, I'm hopeless."

"Let's approach this from another angle."

"I told you I can't do this. I warned you." Kissing still felt like the most unnatural thing I'd ever done. "Our mouths aren't designed for this, are they?" I said. "They're designed for eating and talking, and kissing with them is kind of like trying to use a broom to do yard work."

"Yard work?"

"Yes, yard work. Yard work!"

"You need to calm down."

My hands were cold and I felt dizzy. And Natalie—my friend of several years—was suddenly like a stranger to me. More specifically, I felt like I was seeing a new part of her, which was surprising, considering how well we knew each other, how long we had been friends. I was seeing a more private side of her. It just made me more anxious.

"Is it possible I'm allergic to kissing? Could I be experiencing anaphylactic shock right now? Does my face look puffy?"

"Okay, you just need to relax. We've barely started. I had to see where you stood, that's all. I just needed to see where we were starting from. You haven't done anything wrong."

"What you really mean is that I haven't done anything right."

"I mean you haven't done anything that everyone hasn't done while learning. You didn't learn to drive a car in two minutes, did you?"

I shrugged. "Three or four minutes," I said.

"I'm just saying that you can't expect to learn how to do it without practice."

"Hold on," I said, holding up a finger. "Your analogy has just brought a depressing thought to my head: I learned how to drive at sixteen, but I still don't know how to kiss."

"Shut up," she said. "Come back here." She put my hands back on her. "I have an idea. I heard about this somewhere. Say 'olive.'"

"Olive." For some reason, this made me smile. She smiled back.

"Now we'll both say it while we kiss."

"Talking and kissing at the same time?"

"Okay, let me rephrase: don't even think about the kissing part. All I want you to do is say 'olive' when our lips meet. Okay?"

"Okay."

"Ready?"

"Ready."

"'Olive,'" we both said. The word was muffled by the kiss.

"Now what?" I said. "'Potato'? 'Couscous'?"

"It kinda worked," she said.

"How so?"

"Saying 'olive' mimics a very basic kissing move. The lips part softly, the tongue comes forward, the lips move back together softly."

"Hm."

"In other words, do it again."

We did it again. Then again. Then we staggered the "olives" so that we weren't saying them simultaneously. That worked a little better. She rearranged my hands for me to give me some other typical positions to practice, and we moved a bit closer. For the first time I noticed her perfume—a smell I had only been fleetingly aware of in the past, but now here it was, right in front of me.

"Now say 'olive' without actually saying it," she instructed.

"Say it silently?" I said.

"Yeah, just make the movements with your lips and mouth, but don't say it."

No problem. It worked just as well as before, and now our kissing was silent instead of being a goofy string of garbled "olives."

Our kisses grew longer. She instructed me on breathing through my nose. She talked about noses and how to make sure you didn't bonk straight into your partner's nose. She talked about what she called asymmetry: that in a good kiss, the partners' lips meet *slightly* off target, just a bit high or low or to the side. While she was talking technique, I was noticing how soft the skin of her upper arm was beneath my palm. I looked at her eyes and I could see a tiny reflection of myself there, and behind the reflection—in the black of her eyes—there was Natalie, right in front of me. There was warmth between us wherever we were touching or close.

We decided to try other words in lieu of *olive*. We tried *melon, turnip, squash,* and *apple.* We branched away from fruits and vegetables and tried *brown sugar, provolone, mahi mahi,* and *meat loaf.* We picked the China Wok menu off my desk and tried *moo goo gai pan, crab rangoon, egg foo young,* and *happy family.* We did a whole series of flowers: *geranium, nasturtium, statice, dandelion, dianthus, pansy,* and *poppy.* We did makes and models of cars: *Ford Focus, Mercury Mystique, Dodge Grand Caravan, Porsche Boxter, Honda Pilot.* We did states and their capitals, working our way page by page through the atlas. We picked names at random from the phone book. We did all the listings for the last name Dixon, all the listings for Jacobson, and all the listings for Malloy. Some of the words we said aloud, some were silent.

Finally she told me to stop thinking of words in advance. I could think of them silently on my own if I wanted to but improvise by mixing them up. She, on the other hand, would just kiss me normally, without thinking of words at all.

So we just stood there, kissing. After a while it stopped feeling like I was *practicing* kissing Natalie. It felt like I was actually doing it.

And it was in this way, finally, that at eleven fifteen she pushed me away. "Whoa," she said. "That's getting personal." She fanned her face like she was hot.

"Sorry," I said.

"I mean that it's getting really good."

"Oh!"

"Pretty darn good. You're a natural talent."

I smiled. But I wanted to keep kissing her.

"What words were you saying?" she asked.

"I wasn't, actually," I said. "I guess I was just kissing you like a regular person." I smiled. She smiled. Then she stood up, hugged me, and shook my hand.

"Congratulations," she said. "You've graduated."

And then she left.

Once she was gone, I felt a strange sadness. I was proud of myself, but mainly what I was feeling was that I wished she were still here.

Something had changed.

chapter 16

THE DAY I FIRST MET Natalie, she threw up on me. We were twelve, and we were both attending a summer science camp run by students from the university. But it was less about letting the kids have fun with science and more about recruiting them into some kind of hippie army. In other words, we spent the summer visiting the landfill, the sewage-treatment plant, a tiny strip of restored prairie out by the interstate, the university's "herbarium," and at least three organic farms.

On the first day at camp, on a visit to a farm out in West Branch, we were ushered into the kitchen of a big, dingy farmhouse. It was hot inside and there was a shirtless guy in there washing his sandals in the sink. And the place smelled like old kitty litter. Macie—our natty-headed counselor—had laid out a sampling of the farm's goods, and we each got a little handful of strawberries and a glass of milk. We'd all just met each other an hour ago, and we weren't really talking yet, and Natalie, in front of me, just chugged down her little glass of milk. I sniffed mine, but it smelled a little fusty and it was warm, so I put it down and just ate the berries. Macie was going on and on about the berries and how they were grown in raised mulch beds without pesticides or chemical fertilizers, and then she started talking about the milk and how it came from grass-fed, free-range goats. And the moment we learned that it was goat's milk, Natalie simply turned and spewed. On me.

The next day we were at the sewage-treatment plant, and we had just gotten a tour from the assistant facility engineer. We were walking back up toward the parking lot, and Natalie and I were at the tail end of the group and the engineer was beside us and he said to us, "Remember: your shit is our bread and butter."

And without missing a beat, Natalie said, "And my bread and butter is your shit."

From that moment on, we were friends.

We did, though, have different reactions to the camp. I loved it. I soaked it up and by the end of the two weeks I had stopped eating meat (except olive-oil-packed, line caught, Italian tuna), was lobbying my parents to sell the Cherokee and buy a Geo Metro, and refused to drink any kind of soda but Blue Sky, from Santa Fe.

Natalie, on the other hand, resisted everything. After the presentation on the evils of processed meats, she began bringing bologna sandwiches in her lunch. She gave Macie a gift of some shampoo and a razor. And on the last day of the camp she passed out free lottery tickets to everyone, in defiance of the lecture about the lottery being an unfair tax on the underclass.

Macie won fifty dollars.

As I walked to school, I thought of Natalie. I had dreamed of her all night in an exhausting kind of way. The dreams were basically just her face hovering an inch or two in front of mine. Had I ever spent so much time so close to someone's face as I had last night? No. And now that I was awake, I couldn't get her face out of my mind, and that was fine with me.

The brilliance of Natalie's strategy, I realized, was that by making me think of words instead of kissing and by laughing with me at the silliness of it all, I had basically forgotten that I was kissing her at all. That amazed me. *She* amazed me. She always had. What really surprised me, though, was that near the end of last night, right before she ended the lessons, I had stopped thinking about anything at all. I had stopped thinking because I had started simply enjoying it.

What if, I wondered, the real answer to my girl problems was right in front of me the whole time? I remembered last week when I had lost my favorite T-shirt and spent twenty extremely aggravating minutes looking for it only to realize that I was *wearing* it. Well, what if that's what was going on now with me and Natalie? I didn't quite know, but I wondered.

So I felt good as I ambled toward school, even though it was a warm, humid morning. It was going to be hot today—above ninety—way above normal, but I felt great.

Percy worked as a parking-lot attendant early on Wednesday and Friday mornings, so he couldn't give me a lift today. And I liked the walk—I had a game where I would pick which houses I would live in when I grew up. Childish, yes, but I'd done it for years. There was the little bungalow on Washington Street. The one with all the hosta plants. Very nice. Then there was the big farmhouse on College Street—with a backyard for the kids.

At school they were handing out the school newspaper at the front door. I took one as usual, mainly because I liked to read Ada

Smith's comic strip, *Blatt!,* which was about puppets who were controlled by robots. The robots made the puppets do a lot of dancing.

Normally I ignored the front page, which usually contained headlines about whether students should have more parking spaces. Today, though, I *was* the front page. There was a massive photo of me—thankfully a much better one than Natalie had posted on the web—followed by this story:

JACK BE NIMBLE (JACK BE QUICK)
CHS SENIOR DATES 24 GIRLS IN 7 DAYS
BY JESSICA WOO

Ah, it's prom season again. You can smell the angst in the air. Limousines have been booked. The famous Hummer limousine in Davenport has been reserved since last September. Dinner reservations have been made at 126, Givannis, and Three Samurai. (FYI, the hip un-hip restaurant this year is the Beefstro, in the Coralville Ramada Inn.) Tuxes have been rented. Hairdos selected. Post-prom parties carefully planned. And, of course, couples have, well, coupled. Sad news, girls: all the good guys are taken. All four. (Five if you count Mr. Engle.)

But wait! What ho? Hark and lo! Who is this dark knight on the horizon? Who is this Johnny-come-lately with an anti-cool haircut and a fabulous smile? Who is Jack Grammar, and why won't he go to the prom with me?

Beep, beep, beep. Let's back up. Late last Friday a

personal ad was posted in the online version of this very publication. (It's reprinted below for those very few of you who haven't seen it.) Jack Grammar was looking for a prom date, it seemed, and he wanted to cast a wide net.

Our sources discovered his ad has received over 200 responses, from which he will eventually select 24 girls to go on actual dates with (the selection process is ongoing, so don't give up hope yet). This list of 24 girls—locally referred to simply as "the list"—has been kept private, but yours truly has dug up several names, including Laura Gilden, Celia Proctor, and Chance Mc-Namee. Obviously this ain't no collection of amateurs or no-names. It seems Mr. Jack has his pick of the picks.

How did Jack go from being the slightly geeky kid who could name all thirty-some Shakespeare plays to suddenly being the flavor of the moment? Heck, I don't know. I don't even understand gravity. It's true he looks like Leo before the bloat set in. It's true that he's a cool and perfect six feet tall. It's true that he's headed to the Ivy League in the fall. I've even heard that he has a spunky little sidekick dog. There are other unsubstantiated rumors I can't print here. But maybe the real answer to Jack's allure is that he's genuine, he's honest, and he's just damn cute.

What's Jack looking for? We plead ignorance. Brains and beauty or just T and A? Is he a party guy or a gentleman? Boxers or briefs? Sushi or steak?

So let the games begin! With only a few days left,

we're opening up an online forum where you can get all the latest gossip and news about Jack Grammar and his quest. Contributions are welcome. Check out the handicap board, where our experts rate each candidate's chances. Spread rumors in the chat room. And if you want to throw your hat into the ring, we've got a link to Jack's personal e-mail. The word on the street is that he's allowed to date people not on the list.

Which reminds me. Hey, Jack: call me.

"Strangely enough," I told Julie Vanderwoude at lunch, "I don't mind it." She'd asked me how I felt about the article. "Who knows what's wrong with me today," I continued, "but it just doesn't seem like a problem."

"Well," she said, "I promise not to tell them anything."

"I've got a better idea," I said. "You could feed them extravagant misinformation. Like, tell them that I will only select a prom date who can speak Dutch."

We were eating lunch in the school's video production studio—which was just a fancy way of saying "the back of Mr. Kloski's room." We weren't really supposed to be here, but Julie was the producer for the school's in-house television show, and she could come here whenever she wanted under the pretense of working.

"Or I could tell them that you're actually looking for someone who will marry you this summer. Wink, wink, nudge, nudge. That'd freak them out."

"Let's agree not to freak them out *that* much," I said.

"I'm sorry," she said. "I shouldn't have said that."

Why was she apologizing?

"No, it's okay. Sounds like a good rumor to start."

Julie wasn't someone I'd ever talked to before, but I knew who she was. She had that whole urban hip-hop look working for her.

"That outfit over at the school newspaper is pretty much a joke anyway," she said. "They don't know how to do journalism. I do like *Blatt!*, though."

I admitted that *Blatt!* was about the only thing I read in the paper.

"Can I tell you a secret?" I asked.

"Sure."

"Ada Smith is on the list."

"You're going to go out with the genius behind *Blatt!*? Lucky."

"You can come with me on the date, I guess."

"Surely that'd just be more awkward than necessary."

She then told me that if I ever wanted to respond to the news-paper schlockmongers, she'd be happy to have me come on her show and set the record straight. Or set it crooked. Whichever I pleased.

"I'll think about that," I said. "That might be great."

"Anytime," she said. Then she leaned in close and whispered, "Can I just ask one thing?"

"Sure."

"I promise not to tell, but, well, are there cameras rolling right now?"

She had a weird sense of humor. "Oh, sure," I said. "A bunch of them."

Her eyes flashed around the room, as if looking for hidden

cameras. But she did it in an obviously jokey way. Not that I got the joke.

"Then maybe we should kiss," she said, "just to give them some good footage."

"Kissing for the sake of good footage?" I said. She was taking this a bit far.

"Do you object to kissing me?" she asked.

Not really, I thought. Julie was great. But I thought of Natalie. Kissing Julie for some reason felt like a betrayal of Natalie. But that was nonsense, of course, and besides, I wanted to try out my newly acquired skills.

So kiss we did, and I seemed to navigate it successfully. It did seem *different,* though, than kissing Natalie. I didn't feel it in my toes.

chapter 17

PROBLEM WAS, ADRIAN SWIFT WALKED into the room while Julie and I were sucking face. It seemed to be her job to make me uncomfortable. She saw us and turned and left. I broke off the kiss with Julie.

"What's wrong?" Julie asked. "Who was that?"

"She's on the list," I said. "But I blew her off and told her that I'd already chosen someone else."

"So?" Julie shrugged. "I guess that means you have to choose me. She thinks you've chosen me."

"Oh," I said. "Hm." But of course, I wasn't going to choose her. We just didn't really "click," Julie and I. I realized that I could definitely cross her off the list, and it made me feel good to be able to narrow things down a bit. But then realizing that, I suddenly felt a little weird. Kissing someone I had no interest in didn't make me feel good at all. On the other hand, the fact that I now *knew* how to kiss did make me feel good. I guess I didn't want to go around using my new skill with just anyone.

.   .   .

The other problem, which was perplexing, was that both Natalie and Percy were absent today. They weren't hanging out on the front steps before classes started. They weren't at lunch. Natalie wasn't in French—the only class we shared. They just weren't here. I felt very much alone. It was fair to say that I was a guy with two friends, and without them high school was significantly more lonely, even though everyone seemed to know who I was now. People were trying to talk to me all the time—mostly people I didn't even know—and it was exhausting. People were talking *at* me, not with me.

"Jack Flash!" some freshman boys called at me in the hallway. "You're Jack Flash!"

"I guess," I said.

"You rule!" they said.

That's the kind of stuff I got all day. Although some of it was basically the opposite. Like:

"Hey, Jack! Can I be on the list? Or actually, on second thought: bite me."

Most people were pretty nice, though, or at least not un-nice.

But I was worried. Were Percy and Natalie in league? Was this double absence planned? It wasn't that uncommon for either one of them to take a skip day—or to stay home sick, of course. But *both* of them? And if they were home, why wouldn't they answer their phones? I tried calling both of them. The last thing I needed was for them to be off planning something new together—a second phase to 24/7. Some horrible finale, some reality-show twist.

Between fourth and fifth periods I was wandering down the hallway, worried about my friends—having just reached Natalie's voice mail for the third time—when someone yelled my name. I was getting used to this.

"Jack!"

I looked behind me, but the hallway was crowded and I didn't recognize anyone. It was just general 24/7 harassment.

"Jack! Wait!"

I looked again. And then the students parted, which was a bad sign. Like a duel was about to take place. I got a sinking feeling in my stomach.

"Jack!"

It was Scott Brader. Wheelchair-bound, sports-badass, fork-throwing, Kaylee-Pritchett-avenging Scott Brader. Suddenly I went cold. I had this fleeting vision of blood splattered on the cinder-block wall. Even in a wheelchair, I was pretty sure he was faster and stronger than me. So this was how it was going to go down: in broad daylight, in the middle of the school. Someone would probably videotape the whole incident and my death would later be the topic of a crappy *Dateline* report about violence in the schools and how no one stepped in to help poor Jack Grammar, who was on the honor roll and had never hurt anybody (except a few girls who hated his guts for various reasons) and had once been the vice president of the Stamp Club.

That time Scott pushed me off the jungle gym—ten years ago—I had begged for mercy in vain. I remember him holding my arms tightly, cutting off the circulation, about to push me off, and I stared up at his face and the clouds were racing across the sky and I begged and begged. But over I went, landing so hard on the rubber safety mat that I peed a little bit in my jeans.

This time, I decided, I would beg harder. It was my only hope. Or: flee.

Yes, flee! Flee, flee, flee!

No time to think. Scott was rolling toward me like a gladiator in his chariot.

I gave a wave—a *general* wave, a *nonoffensive* wave, an *apologetic* wave—as a sign of goodwill and to signify that I was in a hurry. Also, I think it was a wave of surrender. Don't worry, I was signaling, I wouldn't be bothering Kaylee Pritchett anytime soon. I learned my lesson. Then I turned and walked as fast as I could. I had to get out of here immediately.

"Hold on!" Scott called. I headed for the nearest stairs—some path that the wheelchair couldn't follow—and finally I reached them, putting some distance between me and Scott. I waited at the bottom of the stairs, trying to catch my breath—which didn't even make sense; I mean, I was a runner and suddenly I was out of breath because of some stairs and a brisk walk? Of course, my escape took me in the opposite direction of my next class and I had to do a crazy roundabout route, at full speed, just to make it on time.

But I'd escaped. Ha! And it was sweet, so sweet.

I walked home right after school. Two carloads of girls passed me and honked and screamed. I gave them a little smile, which just seemed to make them scream louder. Two minutes later the same cars passed me again. They'd circled the block.

"Jack! Give me *babies!*" one of the girls screamed, hanging out the window.

"I don't know how!" I called back, and the girls laughed and I hoped that meant they would stop harassing me.

A grandmotherly woman was kneeling in her tulip bed nearby. We looked at each other and I realized she'd witnessed the exchange I'd just had with the girls.

I shrugged for her benefit. "Girls," I said, by way of explanation.

"I'll say," the woman said.

"I just want a quiet life," I said, "but they won't let me."

I checked my e-mail at home and there was a short e-mail from FancyPants. It was from this morning, from before school started.

Jack—

I've been thinking, and I decided you should be careful. I'm starting to wonder about the motives of some of these girls. I'll get back to you with more.

FP

Hm. Heck, I wondered about my own motives. What was she implying? Whatever it was, it seemed pretty clear that her romantic feelings for me had faded. Her tone was so businesslike now. Apparently I had a knack for scaring away girls whom I'd never even *met*.

I didn't have time to dwell on it, though. And I didn't have time to change clothes at home. Yesterday my sister Hetta had asked me if I wanted to babysit for her this afternoon, and I said sure, of course. No problem. I figured it would be a welcome change from all the breakneck dating. Maybe I wasn't all that comfortable with or fun around girls, but I was around kids.

But when I pulled into the driveway of Hetta's big storybook house, I noticed a lot of cars parked on the street in front of the house. That didn't seem normal. I knocked on the back door and there was no answer and so I just let myself in. It was strangely quiet in the big house. With Hetta's three kids and Jane's little

Rupert over to play all the time, this house was never quiet. Something was wrong.

"Hetta?" I called. No answer.

I walked into the kitchen. Empty. Quiet.

Then Pat the wiener dog appeared from the dining room.

"Hi, pal," I said. "Where's the party?" He licked my shoelaces. Which reminded me: shoes weren't allowed in Hetta's house.

I sat on the bench in the mudroom and took my shoes off. Funny, there were a lot of shoes here—boots, sandals, sneakers— from the size of a Twinkie to a man's size 12.

I walked back into the kitchen. I looked in the fridge. A cake was in there. A whole cake. Weird. Then I heard something in the dining room. Like someone dropped a pen or something. And then I heard Wendy—Hetta's three-year-old—say defensively, "I *am* being quiet."

I stepped through the doorway, the overhead lights came on, and—

"Surprise!!!"

They all jumped up—Hetta, the kids, some girls, and some neighbor kids. In my surprise, I tried to jump backward, but my socks just slipped on the polished wood floor and I fell flat on my back.

"Jack!" Hetta said, rushing to me. "You okay?"

"Maybe . . ." I said.

When my well-being was verified and I was back on my feet, I looked around and saw the five high-school girls. Two of whom I recognized. From the list. In other words: it was a trap. It was a setup.

I'd been had.

chapter 18

IT WAS, TO BE SPECIFIC, a playdate. Or plural: playdates. It seemed that a couple of girls on the list had gotten frustrated because I hadn't returned their e-mails or calls and my schedule was so crammed full of other girls that they had to come up with a scheme to meet me. They'd talked to Natalie, who had talked to Hetta, and bada-bing, the concept of a babysitting gig turned speed-dating session was born. Other girls on the list were notified, and five came. I'd *thought* there were more shoes in the mudroom than usual. More hip, teenage-girl-type shoes.

Natalie, though, wasn't here. Hetta hadn't heard from her since yesterday.

The deal was that each girl got to spend fifteen minutes with me, one-on-one. I sat in the basement and waited for the girls to come to me. Apart from a small laundry room, the basement was just one huge carpeted playroom filled with more toys than was healthy, surely. But despite the array of playthings, the novelty of the day was, of course, not a toy at all, but the metal support pole that stood in the center of the basement, which was, for safety's sake, surrounded by a thick foam sheath to prevent noggin collisions, bone fractures, chipped teeth, and so forth. In fact, Hetta's husband, Ben, had only yesterday added an additional layer of foam, so that the pole was now about as thick as a tree trunk and no matter how hard you hit it, no matter how fast you ran at it, you really couldn't hurt yourself on impact. The kids—Perry, Sami, Wendy, and Rupert, in addition to the neighbor kids Brad and Francine—found this exceptionally amusing and were throwing themselves at the foam pole with remarkable zeal and a good dose of showmanship.

I sat in a beanbag chair nearby. My dates sat in another beanbag chair opposite me.

First off, Jenny Wester. Junior. Cheerleader. Even during summers she spent her time at cheerleading camp. She also liked movies, dancing, hanging out with her friends, and kittens. I told her that in all honesty, I thought those things were pretty fun, too. I asked her what her favorite class was and she asked me to repeat the question.

"Like, which class is the one you look forward to most?" I said.

"Huh," she said, as if it was something she'd never considered before. She shrugged. "Math? Is that the right answer?"

"Well, there really isn't a right or wrong answer per se. I'm just trying to get an idea of what you like, what your favorite things are."

"Oh! Some of my favorite foods are buffalo wings and french fries."

"Yum," I said.

"And pizza!"

"Oh, man, pizza's great," I said. "So great."

"My favorite color is berry."

"Berry?"

"It's kind of half purple and half pink. See?"

She showed me her fingernails, which were indeed painted a berry color. "Very fetching," I said, and as I struggled to figure out how to fill up the remaining twelve minutes in our date, a rubber ball came flying through the air and hit Jenny in the head. It was the kind of ball that didn't hurt.

"Ow!" she said, looking around for the perpetrator. The kids were milling around together, and it was difficult to tell who had thrown it. Then Jenny said an impressive thing: "Which one of you stupid little snot-nosed brats threw that?"

And thus our date ended.

Next came Laura Schiller. Senior. Maybe taller than me. As if to follow up on the ball theme of the last date, Laura immediately challenged me to a basketball shoot-out in the driveway.

"I'm not sure we're allowed to leave the basement," I said. "Plus it's about two hundred degrees out there."

"I'll make it interesting: if I win, you *have* to take me to prom."

"You think I don't know who you are? You think I'm stupid?"

"It's possible," she said.

Laura was one of the starters on the varsity basketball team, which had gone all the way to the semifinals in the state tournament this year. She was All-District, All-State, and was headed to Wisconsin on a scholarship in the fall.

Instead of a shoot-out, we played a little one-on-one.

"You ready for this?" I asked, dribbling in front of her.

She was smiling right at me, crouched in her fantastic defensive stance. "I reckon," she said.

I faked left, went right, and she stripped the ball from me.

"Okay, okay," I said. "You wanna play dirty, we play dirty."

"Oh, we were playing? I thought you were just warming up." She turned around and lobbed the ball effortlessly into the basket.

And my luck didn't change. I thought I could jump higher than her, but I was wrong. She blocked two of my shots. I thought I might be a little stronger than her, but she knocked me over when I tried to make a power drive for the hoop. I thought maybe I could at least beat her from the perimeter, but my shots didn't drop, and hers did.

At the end of it, it was 15–2. She was the best player I'd ever faced. She had fantastically long legs and a nose that had been broken twice and now was slightly crooked—about the coolest nose I'd ever seen. And she kicked my ass thoroughly and easily.

I was pretty much in love with her.

Then came Dee Whalen, a sophomore from Cedar Rapids. She was neat and cute, but I had trouble paying attention to what she was saying. Perhaps it was the fact that I was so sweaty and exhausted from my basketball match, or maybe it was the kids yelling in the background as they continued their collision game with the support pole.

Suddenly she asked me if I was confident about the salvation of my soul.

"Say what now?" I asked. Her voice was soft, and I leaned forward.

"I mean do you have a personal relationship with Christ your Savior? Because Jesus is in my heart and I want you to know what a caring and supportive partner he is."

Was Jesus her boyfriend? Because that's what it sounded like.

I had to basically tell her we really weren't meant for each other—my parents were married in the Unitarian Church, after all. Not that I didn't respect her beliefs, I said. Which was true.

It went from worse to worser. Chance McNamee was the fourth date. Now, there wasn't any denying that she was one of the most beautiful girls in the school. She was one of those girls who already looked like a woman. Why she was trying to get a date with me was beyond me.

"Hi, Jack," she said.

"And hello to you," I said.

"I've been looking forward to meeting you all week."

"That's very flattering," I said.

"It's true."

"But you've met me before," I said.

"I have?"

"Yes."

"But I don't remember. . . ."

"Here's the deal," I said. "In ninth grade, on September 23rd at about ten thirty in the morning, having saved up all my courage for a year, I asked you very politely if you would go to the fall festival with me."

"You did?"

"I did. You were the first girl I ever asked out. And in front of all your friends, you said that not only would you not go to the fall festival with me, you would never go anywhere with me ever, at any time, under any circumstances, no way, no how, nope."

"I said that?"

"You did."

"I did?"

"And I'm going to have to hold you to it."

Bess Eberlee was last. I'd known her since third grade.

"I mean," she said, "I don't get it. I just don't understand the administration. I mean, when the temperature is like, ninety-five, and everyone's just sweating it out and trying to make it through the school day without dying of a heatstroke, they still won't let us bring water bottles to school just because a couple of punks had alcohol in their bottles last year. I mean, is that fair?"

"No."

"How fair is that? It's not fair at all. I need to hydrate. We all need to hydrate. It's a well-known fact that the brain is mostly water, so how do they expect us to learn when our brains are all dried up? And there are lines fifty people long at the water fountains? And we only have five minutes between classes? But you can't drink at the water fountain, and you can't bring a water bottle, and you can't bring a thermos. But you know, those idiots who had alcohol in their bottles, well, they would have brought it anyway, somehow. You know?"

"Yeah."

"I mean, they probably would have smuggled it in their shoes or something. Somehow. In their notebooks. I don't know how. Somehow."

The problem with Bess Eberlee was that even though I liked her, it was difficult to get a word in edgewise. This left you with a lot of time to look at her long red hair and all the perfect freckles on her very smooth arms.

"And it's the same with the dress code. It just doesn't add up.

I mean, when it's this hot, we need to be able to wear clothing that won't make us die of heatstroke, right? We need to wear appropriate hot-weather fashions, right? Especially if they're not going to let school out early. But the administration won't bend on the dress code, and they sent twenty kids home this morning for wearing halter tops and low pants and stuff. I mean, how does that make sense? It's not like we're naked. We're just trying to keep cool. If it's that hot, *send us home early at least.*"

"Uh-huh."

"We're just human beings, you know? People."

"Yeah."

"And they'll learn their lesson when the kids start dropping from dehydration and heatstroke. 'Cause it'll happen. What are they going to do next? Require us to wear wool pants? Sweaters?"

"Ha-ha," I said.

"I mean, like that janitor who keeled over this morning. I saw him. He was wearing pants and a long-sleeved shirt and hat and he was out there sweating away pushing the lawn mower and *bam!* he just kind of fell over. That's how hot it was—and that was in the morning, before it got *really* hot—and that's what's going to start happening to students soon if the administration doesn't smarten up. I mean, really, it's not like—"

"Which janitor?" I asked.

"Huh?"

"Which janitor did you see fall down?"

"Mr. K."

That was Mr. Kowalski. Percy's grandfather.

"When?"

"Oh, half an hour before school. I was there early for band, but we—"

"Do you know what happened to him?"

"Well, I heard that Mrs. Brisbee took him to the hospital but that in the car Mr. K. stopped talking and kind of passed out because he had heatstroke or whatever—which is exactly what I'm talking about!—and I heard from Shawn Smith—the geeky one, not the guy on the tennis team—whose mother is a nurse in the ER, that as soon as he got to the hospital, Mr. K. had a heart attack right there and . . . and . . . and . . . that was it."

I stared at her. It took a second to connect.

I jumped up and headed toward the stairs.

"Hey," Bess called. "Where you going?"

"I gotta go," I said.

"But we got six minutes left."

"I owe you six minutes," I said.

"Six and a half!" she called as I disappeared up the stairs. "Six and a half!"

I went down the hallway, passing the kitchen. Hetta and the other dates, minus Chance McNamee, were in there, cutting the cake.

"Where you going?" Hetta asked.

"I'm sorry, but I've got to go." I didn't even stop—just kept walking.

"But we're cutting the cake," Hetta said.

I headed out the door and cut across the lawn. The heat hit me like a hammer and I felt light-headed. I didn't feel good at all. I couldn't catch my breath and I wondered if I was hyperventilating. I could hear my pulse racing in my eardrums. Damn it!

Tucked under the windshield of my car was a note written on

the back of an envelope. The handwriting was sloppy—the note had been scribbled fast.

> *I'm mean, sorry about your fragile ego and everything else, but I'm here doing you a favor and you're rude to me? Forget you. (That won't be hard.)*

It was obviously from Chance McNamee. I got in the car and read it again. My mind was swirling. Who the heck did she think she was? Suddenly I just felt this anger rise up out of me. I mean, I could understand her being upset that I was a little brisk with her, but what did she mean, she was doing me a favor? How high was her opinion of herself? Why'd she want to go to the prom with me if she looked on it as some kind of act of pity? It was all just so stupid and petty. I hit the steering wheel. The horn sounded. I threw the note out the window and started the car.

After all, Chance McNamee didn't mean anything right now. I drove fast, and I had to make myself pay close attention to the road. My mind was buzzing and scattered and that made it difficult to drive. I felt like I'd done something wrong—that I should have known, or found out, that Percy's grandfather had gone to the hospital—that he'd *died* in fact. Obviously that was why Percy was absent today.

Percy's house was down near Highway 6, in a scrappy neighborhood of small houses, and when I finally pulled up to the curb there, I noticed there were no cars in the driveway. I rang the bell at the front door. There was no answer. So I walked around the side of the house and opened the gate in the chain-link fence and let myself in. The two beagles, Ran and Dan, charged up to me, happy to see me, and jumped up on me. I saw that their water bowl was empty. I filled it, and then I went to the back door. There was a sheet of paper taped to the inside of the glass. The handwriting was Percy's. It just said: *Lloyd—ICU*.

Lloyd was one of Percy's older brothers. This note was left for him. And the ICU—intensive care unit—was presumably where Mr. Kowalski had been?

I knocked on the back door, just to make sure no one was home, but then I headed out.

chapter 19

PERCY AND I ATE DINNER together in the hospital cafeteria. Without the note on the back door, I never would have found him—the university hospital was way too big, and I doubted I could have gotten any information about where Mr. Kowalski was because I wasn't a relative. I'd found Percy along with his brothers and grandmother exactly where the note had said to look. Mr. Kowalski, it turned out, had probably had one heart attack yesterday—a smallish one, or at least one that didn't knock him flat. And this morning he'd had another one just as the vice principal had brought him into the ER. The second one was bigger, but not big enough. Mr. K. was alive. Very sick, but alive.

Percy and I didn't talk much during dinner. The cheeseburgers were pretty good, and I commented on that, but I noticed that Percy was just nibbling at his. I was feeling like a sack of shit for being wrapped up in my own little fantasy world all day and not knowing what was going on with Percy. There I was, kissing girls, going on speed dates in my sister's basement, playing basketball, while Percy was here waiting for news about his grandfather, help-less. And I felt helpless, too.

"If there's anything I can do . . ." I said to Percy when we were done eating. "You know."

"Yeah," he said. "Thanks."

"I mean it."

"I know."

I noticed a girl wandering around on the far side of the cafeteria. "Hey, isn't that Penelope?" I said.

It was, and we called her over, and she and Percy hugged, and I could see him kind of melt in her arms and then I saw that he was crying. I'd never seen him cry.

Percy insisted on staying at the hospital. I asked him if he'd told Natalie about his grandfather and he said no. I asked if he wanted to see her and he said yes. I knew Penelope was a real comfort to Percy, but he and Natalie also had the kind of quiet connection that I knew he needed right now. Emotional connection. Over the years Percy had always talked with Natalie about things he barely mentioned to anyone else—the crap he got from his brothers, the girlfriend who cheated on him, the time he got arrested for shoplifting. She had a way of helping him through his darkest days. His instincts whenever he was hurt were to shut himself off, but Natalie could draw him out.

I called Natalie from the hospital, but she still wasn't answering. I didn't understand. I'd called her several times during school and four times since school got out. I tried her line at her dad's house. Finally I looked up her mom's number and called her. Her mom answered and I identified myself and asked her if Natalie was home.

"Yeah, she's here. She was home all day sick."

Sick? That made me wonder. Did our kissing lessons have anything to do with it? Or was she too embarrassed or ashamed to face me?

"Is she okay?"

"It's just a little stomach thing. She's fine. Dan was here a while ago, so she must not be too sick."

"She's not answering her phone," I said.

"Really? Maybe she's asleep."

"I've tried several times today. I'm surprised Bridget didn't answer, at least."

"Bridget's at a track meet," her mom said. "Do you want me to go get Nat?"

I explained the situation with Percy's grandfather and that Percy would like her to come to the hospital if possible and Natalie's mom said maybe I should just come over and get her. Her house was only a couple of minutes from the hospital.

When I got there, Natalie was waiting for me outside. Her mother had told her what was going on. She got in the car. She did look a little sick. She looked tired. Her face was a little blotchy.

"Let's just head over there right now," she said.

"Okay."

"Is Mr. K. all right?"

"Not so good," I said. I gave her a brief report. "How are you?" I asked. She didn't say anything. "I was worried about you today," I said.

"Sorry," she said. "God, it's hot."

At the hospital Percy and Natalie decided to take a walk outside. It was something I'd asked him if he wanted to do with me earlier, but he'd said no. It was good for him—he'd been in the hospital all day—and they'd have a chance to talk. He and Natalie walked west, toward University Heights, and me and Penelope sat by the main entrance to the hospital. The heat of the day was just starting to ease off. The sun was getting low.

"So how's the twenty-four/seven thing going?" Penelope asked.

"Argh!" I said. "Next question."

"I'm sorry," she said.

"No, I'm sorry," I said. "I didn't mean to snap at you."

"It's understandable," she said.

"I just think the whole thing is so stupid. And I'm not sure it's working."

"What do you mean? Sarah Shay, for one, really digs you. I mean, she asks me about you about every two hours, wondering if you're going to pick her."

"I like Sarah," I said. I shrugged. "But what's that mean? I've met so many girls, and I like a lot of them, and they're all cute and everything, and some of them are really fantastic people. But how am I supposed to pick? I've met at least five girls who are really cool, and I could see myself having fun with them at the prom and everything. But isn't there more to it than that? I need to get to know them more, I guess. But it's just too many choices. And what's it mean about adult relationships? You meet someone you like and you hang around with them and you get along pretty good and so you call it love and you get married? Is that it? It just seems so random. Circumstantial. Like it could be anyone."

"Sounds like you've had a long day."

"You seem really happy with Percy. And I know how happy he is with you. So how do you know he's the one? How do you know for sure?"

"Intuition?" she said.

"But my intuition sucks!" I said. "I can't trust it."

"When you love someone, you *build* a life together. It's work, but it's beautiful. You create something."

"But don't you see what I mean about it being circumstantial and random? I could build a life with a lot of different girls."

"That's illegal."

"You know what I mean."

"I do. I do," Penelope said. "I guess I don't really know much, but look at Mr. and Mrs. K. I mean, they've been married for, what, fifty-five years? And it's not like they've had easy lives. And when they're with each other, they're laughing half the time. Together. They find joy in each other. And . . . You didn't go to the prom last year, did you?"

"No."

"But you know that Mr. and Mrs. K. go every year and that they start the first dance every year."

"Yeah. My sisters talk about that from their proms. My *mom* remembers that from thirty-some years ago."

"Last year was the first time I saw them at the prom. Before I even knew Percy. And when Mr. and Mrs. K. got out on the dance floor and started dancing, they just glowed, you know. They both just lit up, and you could feel it. I swear, you could feel their love. It was overflowing. That's what it was. It was amazing to see them. It still is."

I nodded. "Guess they won't be dancing this year."

"No. But don't you see what I'm saying? That *that's* the goal. What they have. Maybe we're too young to know how to get there. But we can strive to achieve that. That's what we can do."

She was right. I looked at her. "Hey," I said. "You're not FancyPants, are you?"

She shook her head. "No, Jack, I'm definitely not your FancyPants," she said. "Sorry."

"Just asking."

"But"—and she tugged the waist of her skirt to show a strip of neon underwear—"I *am* Fancy Panties."

chapter 20

NATALIE AND I WERE DRIVING east across town as night set in. We'd left Percy and Penelope at the hospital.

"Can we turn off the AC?" Natalie asked.

"Sure," I said.

"I know it's soupy outside, but at least it feels real, you know. Soupy but real."

We rolled down the windows, and the night air came in.

"I feel like such a dumbass," I said. "All wrapped up in myself while Percy was sitting in the hospital all day. And you were home sick and I didn't know."

She didn't say anything, but that was okay. We got out of the car at Percy's house and went around back and let ourselves in with Percy's key. We fed Ran and Dan and filled their water again, and they were so happy they didn't know whether to eat or play, and so they tried to do both at the same time.

Natalie obviously still didn't feel well. She kind of curled up in the passenger seat as I drove her back home. She didn't talk. I felt pretty awkward and weird because of what had happened last night. I didn't know how to think about her. And the way she was acting—so glum—wasn't like her, even if she was sick. Something else was going on.

"You okay?" I asked after we crossed the river.

She made an *umph* sort of noise.

"Tell me what I can do to help you . . ." I said. "Do you have any dogs I can feed? Stuff like that?"

"No dogs," she said.

"But you do have a Dan of your own, come to think of it," I said. Dan the man.

"Actually," she said, "I don't."

"Huh?"

"I don't. Not anymore."

She uncurled herself a little bit. We were almost to her house.

"What are you talking about?"

"We had a fight," she said.

"So. You guys have had a fight or two before."

"This was a real fight. This was bad. . . . We broke up."

"Natalie! Jeez. I'm sorry, Nat. I didn't know. Is that why you stayed home today?"

"No. We just broke up a couple of hours ago. After school."

I parked in the drive in front of her mom's front door. I turned off the engine. What Natalie just said was hard to wrap my mind around, and I didn't know what to say yet. I didn't know what to feel. One part of me was confused—what had happened and why had it happened today? There was another even more confused part of me that was suddenly happy because . . . well, because of the way I thought I might feel about her.

"What did you guys fight about?" I asked. "Did he do something stupid?"

"No."

"Then why'd you break up?"

She shrugged. "I told him about last night," she said, looking away, out the window at the dark house.

"What about last night?"

She looked at me. Her face was wet. She was crying. "Kissing?" she said. "Remember? You and I? Me and you? *Us?*"

"Oh," I said, my heart was pounding. "But I thought we weren't going to—"

"Not going to tell anyone, I know, I know," she said. "But I did. It came out."

Did this mean I was responsible for their breakup? Did this mean that Dan would hate me now?

"Let me talk to him," I said. My stomach was starting to hurt, and the words were pouring out of my mouth. "He knows we're just friends. And he's a great guy. He's my friend, too. He knows that it didn't mean anything. Tell him what a colossal dweeb I am, having to learn how to kiss from my best friend. Tell him that."

"I did."

"And?"

"We broke up."

"But why?"

Pause.

"Because he thinks I like you."

"That's ridiculous. Let me talk to him."

"It won't help."

"Why not?"

"Because maybe he's right."

"About what?" My voice sounded strange, like I was someone else.

"Are you listening to me? Are we inhabiting the same conversation at all? He's right that I *like* you, Jack. I *do* like you. Maybe I always have, you dork."

It hit me.

This was not something I'd been expecting. Maybe I should have been. But I wasn't. Not at all.

We'd been friends forever. Sometimes when we took walks on Sunday afternoons, she would hold my arm like she was my date. I was usually the first person she talked to in the morning and the last person she called before she went to sleep. I didn't know how to feel about what she'd just said. Earlier in the day, I'd actually *wished* for her to feel like this. And now that maybe she did, I had no idea how to react. It was too much of a surprise somehow, and it even confused my own feelings for her. This wasn't some fantasy dream world, this was the real world, and I was the real Jack Grammar, and things were not tidy and dreamy and clear.

"Oh," I said.

"Oh," she echoed. "You say 'oh.'"

"But I . . ."

"Yes, that's why I stayed home from school today, because I didn't think I could face you today, because it was stupid of me to do it, because if I do like you then it's a stupid little schoolgirl crush anyway."

"Let's talk about this," I said. "I don't understand."

"Of course you don't." She unbuckled her seat belt. "Forget it," she said. She opened the door and got out.

"Wait," I said.

She slammed the door.

. . .

I sat there. I watched her go into the house. I waited for some lights to come on inside as she made her way to her bedroom, but the house remained dark. I thought of her inside there, in the dark. I was worried. I was worried about her. I was worried about me. I was worried about Percy. I looked at my hands. I looked at the empty leather passenger seat, illuminated by a wedge of light from the street. I didn't know what to do.

Should I have known? Should I have done something different when she told me? Should I have said something different? Should I have told her how much I had been thinking about her? And what was I supposed to do now? Had I just lost one of my best friends? I thought about last night, and I thought about my dreams—her face right in front of mine, her eyes in front of my eyes.

To complicate everything, I knew that Dan was a good guy. Dan was a friend. Or had been.

Finally I drove home.

Anne Laney was there in my driveway, sitting on the hood of her navy Volvo, waiting. We'd had a date arranged for eight o'clock. It was almost eight thirty. She was just sitting there, twirling one of her bright blond curls around and around on her finger. She didn't look too pleased, especially when I told her that I couldn't go, that I was sick and that I probably wasn't even going to the prom. Perhaps I could have been a bit nicer about it. But then, she could have been, too.

She knew more profanities than I did.

chapter **21**

I SAT ON MY BED with my laptop. I checked my e-mail, but there was nothing from FancyPants. I wanted to tell her what was going on—with Natalie, with Percy's grandfather, that stupid note from Chance McNamee. I wanted to talk things through with her. But she wasn't there. I sat there, picking on my hangnails, hoping that she'd show up online. Finally, when my laptop had grown uncomfortably hot on my legs and three of my hangnails were bleeding, I shut down the computer.

I ran. I ran through the muggy night. My mind was an empty shell, my heart was swollen with confusion, but my feet and legs worked well. They were in top shape. They carried me along. I ran fast and it felt good. I passed other runners.

I ran along the river trail all the way south to where it ended by the softball diamonds. I turned around at my favorite sign in town—my favorite piece of found poetry:

OPTIMISTS CLUB

GIRLS SOFTBALL

DIAMONDS

Diamonds! Girls! Soft! Optimists! It sounded too good to be true. It was. It was too good to be true.

I ran north, back up the river, and instead of turning for home, I kept going. Six miles, seven . . .

I was feeling better. I was feeling full of life. I was feeling centered in myself again somehow. It was as if all the clutter of this crazy week had all converged on today and then suddenly been blown aside. The clouds had parted. The sun would shine again. My path was clear. I looked up, and the stars were shimmering through the haze. I was happier than I'd ever been. The answer was before me and it was so simple.

I turned away from the river trail and headed west into the neighborhoods. I went as directly as I could.

I rang the bell.

After a long time Natalie came to the door.

"I ran here," I said.

"You're dripping," she said.

So we kissed, this time for real.

part **3**

chapter 22

THURSDAY. THURSDAY, THURSDAY, THURSDAY. I liked Thursdays. I always had. Not only was I born on a Thursday, but, according to my parents—and why they felt the need to burden me with such disturbing details, I don't know—I was *conceived* on a Thursday. And this Thursday, of all the Thursdays I had ever greeted, seemed like it was *my* Thursday. My day. Mine. I lay in bed after my alarm went off and I looked at the sky through the window and I realized I was smiling.

Percy was going to be at the hospital all day, so I walked to school again. Almost magically, yesterday's heat and humidity had disappeared, and the morning was crisp and cool and basically perfect. The sun shone through the leaves. I walked slowly.

As I came up the front walk of school, Mary Langley-Lola called me over to where she was sitting under one of the pine trees on the lawn. From here there was a nice view of the western sky. Mary was on the list, and she was one of the cutest of the neo-hippie crowd. Her huge, out-of-date glasses only made her more charming. She had two braids and a green canvas tote bag with a whale embroidered on its side. Not a save-the-whales kind of whale, just a cute whale.

This morning she had her guitar with her, and she played me a song that she said she had written for me. She was a good guitar player—classical guitar—and the tune was inviting and warm, and she played it so earnestly and freely that I didn't feel self-conscious or embarrassed. Thankfully, there were no words to this song. It was a beautiful little song and it sounded to me like an ode to the day and to my new life.

"That was wonderful," I said when she was finished.

"I just want you to know that prom doesn't mean much to me," she said. "But that getting the chance to get to know you would be great."

I told her that was very sweet and I appreciated it but now wasn't the time—my prom plans were made. She nodded, very mellow, and said she hoped I had chosen the right girl for me.

I thought of Natalie. I started beaming. I couldn't stop smiling. "I definitely picked the right girl," I said. "I feel so good about it. I feel *great* about it."

The day was like a dream—the perfect weather, the strange calm in me, and Natalie there with me, smiling, eating lunch with me out by the tennis courts.

I'm in love, I told myself. I'm in love, I'm in love, I'm in love. I'd been repeating this silently to myself all day, as if the words were part of the package. This wasn't a feeling I'd had before. I felt safe somehow. I felt more connected: not just to Natalie, but to everyone, everything. I felt, too, an immense sense of relief, like everything would be good from now on, like this was how things were supposed to be, like this was how the rest of my life

would feel. It was like the feeling you get on the first warm day in spring when you can wear shorts for the first time. But this was better.

To top it off, 24/7 was over. It hadn't even ended up being 24/7. It was more of a 16/5.

"I'll wear that black dress," Natalie said at lunch. "The one with the little embroidered flowers."

I knew exactly which dress she was talking about. It was a vintage dress.

"So what's that mean about my cummerbund?"

"Cummerbund?" she said. "Hm. I don't think so. How about you leave the cummerbund at home and go Euro?"

"That's exactly what I should do," I said. "You're so smart." As I said that, it reminded me of something I'd written to FancyPants in an IM a couple of days ago. "You're so smart . . ." I repeated.

"Go tell it on the mountain," she said.

We laughed, and I looked at her. Was she FancyPants? It was possible, wasn't it? It kind of clicked. . . .

"Percy called me this morning," Natalie said.

"Everything okay?"

"Mr. K.'s stronger today," she said. "Percy sounded bet Penelope's over there right now having lunch with him." I'd w dered where she was.

"Isn't this kind of weird and wonderful at the same tim said. I couldn't contain myself.

"What is?"

"This. Us. I mean, yesterday we had no clue, and yo home brooding and I was here wondering and now look a all changed. Just like that."

She nodded and I looked at her and couldn't help smiling. Wonderful as it was, it all still felt a little new. We were a little hesitant. We weren't lovey-dovey or anything. We were sitting a proper distance apart.

"You realize you've used your wild card on me," she said.

"I have?"

"I think so."

"Cool."

There was no one around. We were pretty much done eating. We had a few minutes left.

"So . . . ," I said, "do you want to kiss?"

"Eh, whatever."

"Not that I condone that kind of crap. I'm firmly anti-PDA. At least on school grounds."

"I hear you."

"But," I said, "it's not like there's anyone around. And anyway, we're going to graduate in a few weeks, and then we'll never have a chance to flaunt the rules again."

"Stop it with the rationalizations," Natalie said.

We kissed, and it was nice.

Then out of the corner of my eye I noticed someone passing behind us. I hadn't seen them before, but it meant that they'd witnessed the kiss.

It was Adrian Swift. Who else would it have been?

"Whoops," Natalie said after Adrian was far enough away. That was Adrian Swift, wasn't it?"

"Yeah."

"I wonder why she didn't say hi."

"She hates me. And now I'm guessing she might hate you, o. I rejected her by telling her I'd already chosen someone else.

Then she walked in on me and Julie Vanderwoude kissing. And now she just saw us kissing."

"She'll get over it," Natalie said. "Now tell me the truth," she continued, turning her attention back to the remains of her apple. "On a scale of one to ten, how do I rank as a kisser? Now that you've kissed a few girls."

I thought about it.

"Twelve."

"Don't flaunt the scale, acehole."

"Eleven point five?"

What we did after school was something I'd never really done in my life. We walked home together. That's right, I'd never really walked a girl home. Of course, we walked to my house, not hers, which really wasn't the way it was supposed to work. And when I offered to carry her backpack, first she laughed, then shrugged, then she said, "Sure," and I had to figure out how to carry two full backpacks. I ended up putting one backpack on my front so that I was basically part of a backpack sandwich. She gave me a peck on the cheek.

We rummaged in the refrigerator and I found some leftover chicken, but she thought it was weird that I was eating it cold. She decided not to have anything, but when I broke out the Fig Newtons, we did a number on them together.

We played Gran Turismo on the PlayStation, and we had a battle of the midget cars. I drove some Opel with what sounded like a dying fly for an engine, and she drove a little delivery cart or something and she kept trying to run me off the road, which was comical at her top speed of about forty. The whole race turned into a demolition derby.

We walked Flip.

We made out for nine minutes. And then both of us decided it was time for her to go home.

Having my best friend and girlfriend rolled up in one was about the best thing ever.

Half an hour after Natalie left, I got another e-mail from FancyPants.

> Jack—
>
> The thing is, I've kind of rummaged around and discovered that Celia Proctor was under the impression that you were dying—like you had three months to live or something—and that's why she went out with you and that explains that weird stuff she said about your "situation." Since you're a pretty high-profile guy right now, I'm not surprised that there would be rumors about you floating around, but I just think you need to be careful and make sure whoever you choose as your prom date is honest with you.
>
> How was yesterday? Give me an update on everything and let me know if you want to IM sometime.
>
> > FP

I read the e-mail twice. Then a third time. Two questions were bothering me at the same time. First, why would Celia have heard that I was dying? It was a ridiculous, asinine rumor anyway. Why would she believe it in the first place? I re-read FancyPants's e-mail and thought about it.

The second question, and the more pressing one, was

whether FancyPants was Natalie. On the one hand, why would Natalie still be keeping up the charade at this point? Well, maybe she was still playing out the role, guiding me. Or was she too embarrassed to reveal herself right now? She would wait for the prom, wouldn't she? On the other hand, the timing of the e-mail—half an hour after Natalie left—made sense.

I thought more about it. Yesterday, when I hadn't heard from FancyPants, Natalie had been home "sick" all day, agonizing over me, and it stood to reason that she wasn't in the mood to write perky e-mails to me. And I remembered that time when I was IMing with FancyPants and I had tried to call Natalie and her line had been busy. Because she was online IMing me! Duh!

It *did* click. Natalie had liked me and couldn't tell me and couldn't go to the prom with me, so she entertained her crush on me by flirting with me via FancyPants and doling out advice that she hoped would bring me to her. Like, for example, the suggestion that I had to tell my friends about my lack of kissing experience. Which led me straight to Natalie, of course . . .

And that's why FancyPants seemed to know me so well! And that's why she couldn't tell me who she was or go out with me! And that's why she knew my personal e-mail address!

I felt great. I felt fantastic. It was as if the final piece of the puzzle was in place. The world was complete, and my FancyPants and my Natalie were one and the same.

The stupid rumors about me dying didn't matter now. I was going to the prom with Natalie and so I didn't have to think about this 24/7 mess anymore. There was only one thing left I had to do.

I sat in my room and held my phone in my hand. I was looking out the window at the lawn and the trees. The breeze was blowing through the screen. I could hear the wind chimes tinkling on the back deck.

I turned the phone on and dialed the first number. I got the voice mail.

"Hi, Callie. It's Jack Grammar. I know you haven't heard anything from me all week, but I just wanted to let you know that I've decided not to attend the prom with anyone on the list. I'm going with someone else, someone I've cared about for a long time. I think the list was a mistake and I'm sorry if I've let you down. Anyway, that's all. That's the news. I wanted to make sure you knew and I hope you have a great time this weekend, no matter what you do. Thanks."

I hung up. One down, many to go. I had, on my lap, the phone numbers of everyone on the list. I dialed the next number.

"Hi, is Bess there?" I asked.

And so on. I called everyone that hadn't already been eliminated, including the few I hadn't met yet.

This was what I had decided I needed to do. This was the right thing. 24/7 was officially over. Over, done, concluded, and finished . . .

chapter 23

THEN AFTER DINNER, NATALIE PICKED me up in her mom's convertible. I got in the car and gave her a cheerful peck on the cheek—I kissed FancyPants!—but it didn't even get a smile out of her. Her face was drawn and she didn't look at me. She put the car into gear.

"Hi, Jack!" I said chirpily. "How are you? What have you been up to for the past three hours, Jack, my boy?"

"Hi," she said flatly.

"Oh, I don't know, Natalie," I said, continuing my fake dialogue. "I did a bunch of homework so I could spend the rest of this fine evening with you." Pause. "Really, Jack? That's so lovely."

Something was wrong. She was expressionless, staring at the road.

"I did, actually," I said. "I did my homework."

"Excellent," she said sarcastically.

This was weird. Something wasn't right.

We drove out to Kent County Park. We didn't talk, and on the drive out there, we pulled over and put the top up—the air was kind of cold, especially at sixty miles an hour. We pulled back onto the highway and found ourselves stuck behind a farmer hauling a bunch of pigs in a trailer. We couldn't pass on the curvy road and the smell was very vivid, to say the least, even with the windows closed. Finally we turned into the park. There were some ducks standing in the road, and we waited for them to move, but they didn't. Two cars pulled up behind us. This was a traffic situation all of a sudden. So I got out of the car and shooed the ducks along. They moved, but they quacked at me in a way that was definitely neither polite nor civil.

"I'll teach your grandmother to suck eggs!" I yelled at them.

"Harassing ducks?" Natalie said through her open window.

"Yes," I said. "That's exactly what I'm doing."

Finally she smiled.

We parked by the beach, at the south end of the lake. In a few weeks the beach would be open for swimming, but now it was empty and the sand was smooth.

We walked over the dam and watched a fisherman reel in a little catfish. We turned onto the limestone path and kept walking, and finally Natalie started talking and seemed to be in a better mood. She said a few things about her classes, then complained about Bridget borrowing her favorite lipstick and leaving it on a dashboard where it melted. But before we were halfway around the lake, we'd run out of things to say. We held hands as we walked and then we hiked partway up one of the hills and lay there on the grass so that we had a view of the sunset. The evening was calm and there were high clouds that looked like ribs. The grass was thick underneath us, and pretty soon we were kissing, and then suddenly we weren't and Natalie sat up and said, "I gotta sneeze." She sat there, looking paralyzed, about ready to sneeze, but the sneeze didn't come. "Lost it," she said.

"You're FancyPants," I said. "You were all along." I hadn't planned on bringing this up yet, but I felt like I had to rise to the occasion somehow and bring Natalie out of her mood. I had to reaffirm our connection, and this, I figured, was a charming way to do it.

But she looked at me, and there was a blankness in her eyes. It was as if I didn't know her anymore. Then she got angry.

"Listen, Jack, I'm *not* FancyPants, and I never *was,* never *wanted* to be, never *will* be!"

"Okay, okay. I just thought—"

"No, you didn't think!"

"I—"

"You're fixated on someone who doesn't exist."

"I'm not, I'm really not. I just . . ."

"Just what?"

Yes, just what? I felt suddenly unbalanced.

"I just . . ." I muttered. I felt like the mood had shifted, drastically, badly. I didn't know how to fix it.

"Just nothing," she said. "You're being idiotic."

"I'm sorry," I said. "I don't know what's going on."

"What's that *mean*?" she said. "What the hell do you—" She just stopped cold.

We were both sitting up. Natalie sniffed. She flicked an ant from her arm. Then she looked down at the lake. I plucked a blade of grass.

"I'll tell you what I mean," I said. "A few hours ago you were all friendly and charming and smiling and now you pick me up and you're silent and you don't look at me and you go ballistic when I even mention FancyPants, which—"

"You're living in a fantasy world, that's why."

"And you're not being honest with me. Why have you soured on me in just a few hours? Huh?"

She didn't answer. She looked out at the lake.

"I'll answer for you," I said. Then I said, "Dan."

"What about him?" she said softly.

"You talked to Dan," I said. "Didn't you?"

"Maybe."

"Okay," I said. "Okay, okay. Let's go home."

We drove back into town, and it was getting dark.

I said, "Maybe you should turn the headlights on." She didn't say anything and she didn't turn on the headlights.

She dropped me off at home and I said good night and she just drove away without looking at me. I watched her drive off in the dark without her headlights on and all my energy drained out of me. Things had flipped so quickly. I was all smiles this morning and at lunch we were happy and cute and after school we played video games like best buddies and now it was like we had derailed.

Flip greeted me inside the front door with his tennis ball in his mouth. He dropped it at my feet.

"No ball for you," I said.

He was looking up at me and I got into a staring contest with him that he won and then he picked up his ball and put it down again.

"I said no ball for you!"

Ten seconds later we were playing ball.

I would throw the ball down the long first-floor hallway and he would chase it down. Sometimes the ball would go through one of the doorways, but that just made the game more interesting and gave me more time to wait there with my arms crossed, brooding, before he returned and I threw it again.

I brooded. I brooded old school. I thought about Natalie. I thought about me. I thought about me and Natalie. As if I wasn't confused enough *before* Natalie and I flung ourselves together. Now I was in a new state of confusion, exponentially more confusing than the confusing state of confusion that had come before. Here we were, going on twenty-four hours together, and something was wrong already—extremely wrong.

But what? She *wasn't* FancyPants. Why was that so hard for me to accept? And were her feelings for Dan simply unresolved, or—

The doorbell rang.

I knew it was her at the door. I knew it. I had never been more sure of anything in my life. And so I waited a little bit. I took a breath and held it, then let it go. Everything was going to sort itself out. She had come back to me.

I walked to the front door.

I paused: what would happen?

I opened the door.

It wasn't Natalie.

It was Scott Brader.

"Jack!" he shouted, and my breathing stopped. There he was, wheelchair and all, right on my front porch. It was kind of like opening your sock drawer in the morning and finding a rabid pit bull in there. I thought frantically: Just slam the door shut right now! Just put a dead bolt between yourself and Scott! But I didn't shut the door. I was stunned. I thought of the painless but extremely frightening feeling of that flying fork—those so many years ago—lodging itself in my hair. I thought of that sensation of hitting the rubber mat under the jungle gym and realizing that I had just wet myself. It was all coming back, all at once, and I didn't know what to do. If my mommy had been home, I could have run to her. But I was alone.

And a tall, big-jawed man stood behind Scott. It took me a second to recognize him. Mr. Brader, Scott's dad. The baseball coach. Not only was I about to be beaten by Scott Brader on my own front porch, but I was about to be beaten by a father-son team. It only made sense. This Thursday was going to be the worst Thursday ever.

"Hey," I said. "Guys . . ." How are you supposed to greet your attackers?

"You're a hard guy to track down!" Scott said. "You're not making it easy."

"I'm sorry . . ." I mumbled. "I didn't really mean to. I don't really think we have a problem here, do we? I mean, I don't. I really, really didn't mean to create any problem, and I just want you to know that, and yeah, it's all cool. So, okay?"

I was holding Flip's tennis ball, and as I ended my lame peacemaking speech, I dropped the ball and it bounced into Scott's lap and out of the corner of my eye I saw a blur of fur and I knew that Flip was already airborne. Scott caught the ball, Flip landed in his lap, and the wheelchair rolled backward on impact. If Mr. Brader hadn't been there, Scott would have tipped over the porch steps. Flip, that son of a bitch! My own dog was just making things worse. I really, really, really didn't want to get hit. I really didn't want to be here.

"Wow! This is a great little dog!" Scott said.

Great little dog? I was expecting for Scott to wring Flip's neck and then use him as a weapon against me. Great little dog?

"Shortstop?" Mr. Brader said. "Second base?"

"Uh . . ." I managed to say, "he's more of an outfielder?" Was this conversation really happening? Or was I already dead? "Catching and chasing," I said.

Flip had hopped down with his ball. He dropped it and I picked it up.

"Dad," Scott said, "can me and Jack talk in private?"

Flip barked at me, asking for the ball.

"Not a problem," Mr. Brader said, and he gave me a big-jawed glare and retreated toward the SUV parked at the curb. I felt like apologizing to him that I was just a candy-assed runner and not a baseball player.

Flip barked again.

Okay, *now* here it comes, I thought. His dad has excused himself so he won't have to witness the pummeling to come.

"I want to tell you what's going on," Scott said. "I think you deserve to be filled in. What's happened is that Kaylee is real depressed. I mean, first I broke my ankle and all, which was tough on her. Tougher on her than on me, I think. And then you turned her down cold. Stone cold. That was hard for her. That was real tough. I tried to explain that you probably had already chosen someone or of course you would go with her."

"Uh-huh," I said. I didn't like this. I didn't like that he was explaining the *reasons* for the impending assault.

"But anyway," he continued, "she's real down, and she cut off all her fingernails yesterday, which was a pretty desperate act, you know."

I didn't know what else to say, so I just nodded. I was aware that my mouth was open.

"I know, I know," Scott said. "She gets two manicures a week.

She put so much care into her nails, and then suddenly—snip—
they're gone. So I think that tells you the kind of despair she's
experiencing."

We were getting closer now. Again. I wasn't wearing shoes,
which was a disadvantage. And was it against the rules to try to
tip over the wheelchair? And what about his cast? Could I attack
his cast? Was that allowed? What, after all, were the rules for a
weenie like me in a fight with an injured alpha-male like him? I
hadn't been in a fight since my sisters left home. They'd always
won anyway.

Maybe I could stall. I could just blabber, hope to placate him.

"Sure, sure," I said. "I mean, I feel horrible. I don't think I can
tell you how bad I feel. I really do. I mean, I really, really, really,
really didn't want to hurt her or anything. That's not something
I'd ever do. I'll pay for new nails or whatever. That's not a problem, okay? It's pretty clear that I'm the one to blame here, and I
admit that, and I want you to know that whatever I can do to
help now or to put things right, I'll do it. I'll do it, no problem."

"I'm so glad you want to help. Because you *can* help her, Jack!
Just go to the prom with her. *Please.* She can't be a candidate for
queen if she comes without a date. And all the decent guys but
you are taken, and I could make one of my friends break a date
and go with her, but you know, I really just don't *trust* any of
them. At all. In any way. But I trust you. You're a good guy, and
you're a gentleman, and Kaylee wants to go with you. Since she
can't go with me on account of me being banged up."

"Of course."

"So whaddaya say?"

Er, what? Why hadn't the punching started? Obviously this

was a trap. If I said yes, then *bam!* he'd set me straight and break my skull and tell me never to even think in a million years of laying eyes on her again. If I said no, he'd laugh and point out that of course he was just jerking me around and that there was no way she'd ever want to go out with me and then *bam!*

"Bam . . ." I mumbled.

"What's that?" he asked.

Wait a second. I looked at him. The third option: he was for real. I was just scared because that's what I did best. He wasn't here to beat the hell out of me. He was being serious. He hadn't said anything truly threatening. I'd just chosen to interpret everything that way. I mean, just looking at his face, you could tell he wasn't an actor. He was too simple. My fraidy-cat self had just taken him the wrong way from the start.

"Do you—you . . ." I stammered. I decided to play it straight. To say what I felt. If I was wrong, then I was wrong. "I really appreciate you coming over here," I started, "and letting me know what's going on."

I paused. He was listening. He was listening!

"And of course it's very tempting to say yes," I continued. "And I would like to help Kaylee out. I don't want her to go and cut off her hair or something. But . . . Can I just tell you where I'm coming from?"

"I want you to," Scott said. And then he smiled. He wasn't here to hurt me! O frabjous day! Callooh! Callay!

"Well, you see that when I agreed to this whole twenty-four/seven thing, I told myself that the only way to go about it was to follow my heart. And I've learned that my heart is a confused and fickle organ and that following it is sort of like following a mutt who thinks he smells bacon somewhere in the distance—who knows where you're going to end up? Is there really bacon somewhere or is it just a phantom smell?"

"Bacon?" Scott said. "Phantom smell?" I was getting too poetic for him. Heck, I might as well mention the transgenic forces of springtime.

"What it comes down to is that I have to choose a girl for the right reasons. Because remember, I'm not just choosing one girl, I'm also rejecting twenty-three other girls. And it's my obligation to them to choose someone who means a lot to me. And to be perfectly honest, I've kind of already chosen someone. So, I guess that's it."

He was nodding, downcast. He'd actually thought I was going to say yes. He wasn't angry, though, just a little sad.

"I see what you're saying," he said. "I get it."

"I wish I could help more," I said.

"That's all right. I was just hoping it would work out."

"Call me crazy," I said, "but I think you two should go together even though you're in a wheelchair."

"She'd never go for it," he said.

"Well, have you asked her?"

"No, not officially . . ." he said.

A few minutes later Scott and I were in the kitchen. He was sitting there quietly sipping a Yoo-Hoo I'd given him, and I was on the phone.

"No, it's not because I don't think you're attractive," I explained to Kaylee.

She squawked something back at me. I gave Scott a thumbs-up.

"No, it's not because I'm intimidated by gorgeous women," I said.

"Then what's your *issue?*" she said. "Why'd you tell me off that day? Why'd you call me back and say those things?"

"I apologize for all of that. I do. I was wrong and I was in a bad mood and everything I said was the exact opposite of what I really believed."

There was a pause. "Then why won't you go to the prom with me now?" she asked.

"Because it's not my place to stand between you and the man who loves you."

"What are you talking about?"

"Scott was over here," I said. "And we had a talk."

"Oh my God," she said. "Did he hurt you bad? Are you okay?"

"It wasn't like that," I said. "It wasn't like that at all. Scott's a great guy, and the whole reason he came over here was to convince me to go to the prom with you. That's how much he cares for you: he just wanted to make you happy, to help you get what you wanted. Now, if he knew that I was telling you this, I'm sure he'd pulverize me."

I looked at Scott. He gave me a thumbs-up this time.

"He asked you personally?" she said. "Like you were one of his peers?"

"Yes," I said. Peers? She knew the word *peer?*

I heard her snuffle a little bit. This was working.

"Just think how big a man it took to do that," I said. "And of course because of his wheelchair his dad had to drive him over here and roll him up onto my porch, like he's some Cub Scout selling popcorn."

"Scott did that for me?"

"I know this whole prom thing has been tough for you, what with Scott's broken ankle and everything. But I just wanted to tell you what he was doing for you, and I thought perhaps it would help you reconsider everything. He's the man for you, and that's all there is to it."

"Yeah . . ." she said. I could practically hear her dabbing her tearful eyes to prevent mascara runs.

"And another thought occurred to me," I said. "If you took Scott to the prom, people would think you were a hero." This wasn't in the script. Scott was looking at me curiously.

"A hero?"

"Because you'd basically be making a statement about"—I did some quick thinking here, dumbing it down for Kaylee—"how beautiful and capable handicapped people are."

"Oh!" Kaylee said.

"And I think that would go over real well with the prom queen voters . . ."

"Oh!" Kaylee said. "I'm going to call him. I'm going to call him tonight!"

"That makes me happy," I said. "I think it's the right thing to do."

After I hung up, Scott was looking expectantly at me.

"Well?" he said.

"Not only do I think she's now receptive to the idea," I said, "but I don't even think you're going to have to ask her. She's going to ask you."

chapter 24

I WAS FEELING GREAT after Scott left. I was a genius. I marched around the kitchen in my socks and repeated, "I'm the great communicator!" over and over again in an announcer's voice. Mom and Dad came in with a bunch of groceries.

"I'm the great communicator!" I said.

"Actually," Dad said, "your SAT verbal scores weren't that outstanding."

"You're an *above average* communicator," Mom said.

"Ow! My own parents don't believe in me!"

"Here," Dad said, "put these groceries away," and he went back to the car to get more.

"Oh," Mom said, stopping by the sink, "was Natalie here?" She picked a half-empty glass of soda from the sink. That was something Natalie always did—leave her half-empty glass in the sink.

"Yeah," I said. And my good mood evaporated.

I crept up to my room. I sat at my desk, then I lay on the bed, then I rolled onto the floor. The carpet wasn't very clean. There were crumbs on it.

The thing was, I could understand that Natalie had strong feelings for Dan. That's just how damn sensitive and understanding I was. I could even support her affections for Dan if I had to. What was *really* bothering me were my own feelings. Why had I been so disappointed so quickly as soon as I discovered that Natalie wasn't FancyPants? Shouldn't it not have mattered? Shouldn't it not have mattered at all?

Yet somehow it did. Maybe Natalie was right that I was simply living in a fantasy world. Maybe I was so excited about the possibility of having found such a perfect solution that I convinced myself I felt something different than I did.

It would have been so perfect.

The phone rang. I looked at it. If it hadn't been within arm's reach, I wouldn't have bothered to answer it.

"Hi," said Natalie.

"Hey," I said.

She sniffled.

I didn't know what to say. I said, "I'm lying on the floor."

She didn't say anything.

"So . . ." I said. "Hello?"

"Sorry," she said. "I'm spaced out."

"You called *me*," I said. "You drove away with your *headlights* off."

She hung up. I realized I'd spoken the last sentence like an accusation.

I lay there, cradling my phone against my face. Then I sat up and I cried. I wasn't even sure why I was crying exactly. I was just suddenly very, very tired. I hadn't cried in a long time and I did it silently and it hurt—my stomach cramped up. And I didn't have any tissues in my room. I ended up blowing my nose in a dirty T-shirt. Finally I ducked down the hallway to the bathroom and washed my face. I cupped my hands and drank from the faucet. That made me feel a little better. I went back to my room.

My phone rang again and I let the voice mail get it. I waited, then listened to the message.

"Okay," Natalie said, "I'm just telling you that I'm sending you an e-mail."

I got online and checked my e-mail, but there was nothing and so I stood up and closed the window and then took off my socks—which were filthy—and then checked my e-mail again and there it was.

> I'm not sure how to do this and I don't know if you even want to hear from me, but I know I should tell you something concrete. I think it's clear that this isn't right—each of us wants to be with someone else. I still want to be with Dan, even though I don't know if that's really a possibility at this point. We made a mistake, Jack—we were trying to force something that wasn't really there.

So that was it. It was over even more quickly than it had begun. I read the message a few times and then deleted it from my mailbox. I didn't want it there. It was just evidence of a mistake. Natalie and I were clearly destined to be friends, nothing more, and whatever madness and misalignment of the stars had made us leap into a romantic entanglement was impossible to explain.

Mostly I felt emptied out. I felt like I had just finished a long race and come in last. But at least it was over.

It was to be a night of surprise visits. That's just the way it was. After an hour of reading and taking notes, I heard the doorbell ring. Mom called up to me and said Dan was here to see me.

Dan. My buddy, who had every right to hate me. Perhaps he would deliver the pummeling that Scott Brader had not.

He was sitting on the trunk of his car, hands in his jacket pockets. He smiled when he saw me and he patted the trunk next to him. He looked sad. I'd never seen him without that little-boy gleam in his eye.

I sat next to him.

"You know," I said, "that kissing stuff was stupid of us, but I want to assure you that it was completely innocent."

He nodded. "I know. I'm the one that got it all wrong. I blew it out of proportion. I screwed up."

He screwed up? Of the three of us, he was the one least to blame. I wanted to be honest with him now. I wanted to be able to tell him how things had happened, but it wasn't really my place to do it. It was Natalie's, in her own time.

"Natalie and I go way back . . ." I said, but I didn't know where that was heading, and I trailed off.

"I know," Dan said.

"How can I help?" I said.

He shrugged. "I'm just scared, I guess," he said. "I don't know whether to call her or go to her house or just leave her alone. I don't know how to apologize."

"I don't think there's a wrong way to apologize. As long as it's sincere, which I know it is."

"I already apologized once," he said. "But not to her face. I wasn't brave enough for that."

"When?" I asked.

"Yesterday," he said.

"What did you do?"

He reached in his back pocket and pulled out a piece of paper. It looked like a parking ticket.

"It's a citation for vandalism," he said.

I couldn't help laughing. Some romantic Dan stunt had gotten him a ticket. "What?" I said. "How'd you get this?"

"You know that really steep street as you drive to Natalie's house?"

"Sure."

"I spray-painted a message on it in huge letters, running straight up the center of the street. Of course, I did it in broad daylight and I ran out of paint in the middle of it and when I came back with more paint, the cops were waiting for me."

"This is a two-hundred-dollar ticket," I said.

"I know, and I didn't even get to finish the message."

"What did it say?"

"It was supposed to say 'I'm sorry, Natalie,' but it says 'I'm sorry, Na.'"

"But I'm sure she got the idea. I'm sure she knew what it meant."

"Do you? Did she say anything to you about it?"

"No," I said. But I realized that it was why her mood changed yesterday after she went home. I patted Dan on the shoulder.

"I don't need to stand in the way of anybody," Dan said. "And I want you to know that Natalie should be with whoever she thinks is right for her. You're a great guy, and . . . and . . . I just wanted to say that."

"Dan, Dan, Dan," I said. "You're my hero. But I don't think you've got anything to worry about. I just got an e-mail from Natalie an hour ago, and you're who she's thinking of. That's all there is to it. End of story. She still wants to go to the prom with you."

He looked at me, at first with disbelief, then with relief, then with joy. "Really?" he said.

"Really," I said.

"But what about you?" he said.

I waved him off. "Me? Don't worry about me. I'll be okay."

At least I hoped I would be. Somehow delivering the good news to Dan, which made him so happy, simply brought my depression to a head. I slunk to my room and turned on the WB. I thought I'd had everything figured out, that being with Natalie was the answer. But it obviously wasn't, because it was over.

What hit me now, as I slumped in front of the TV, was that I'd mucked up other people's lives. Natalie and Dan, for one. And the girls on the list, I knew some of them were hurt. That freshman, Samantha Milligan, who had cried. Celia Proctor—egomaniac that she was—whom I had been a bit mean to. And the girls who I turned down flippantly. I'd been so sure I'd found the right thing. I'd been so sure that *this* was going to be *it*.

I'd had such high expectations, of course I was disappointed.

And maybe it was the same with prom. Maybe it was the same with everything.

All my life I'd looked into the future and thought, hey, things are going to be great then. *Then.* Like, hey, once I get to junior high, everything's going to be cool and people are going to be smarter and nicer and my life will really start. And later, hey, once I get to high school, everything's going to be cool and people are going to be smarter and nicer and my life will really start. Well, junior high was over, and it hadn't been the wonderland I'd hoped it would be. Now high school was nearly over, and it had been basically the same as junior high but with cars. And college was next. Now I was dreaming about college, fantasizing about what it would be like and how it would be great and how I would finally be in a place that I loved. But I knew it would turn out just the same: it would just be another insipid popularity contest.

So I made these resolutions: I would apologize to Natalie, Dan, Samantha Milligan, and everyone else on the list. I would stop fantasizing about how great college would be. I would stop looking for the one thing that would solve everything.

And I *would* go to the prom with someone. High school was nearly over, but it wasn't over yet. It could still turn around. But I had to make the effort.

I got online and e-mailed everyone on the list that 24/7 was being un-canceled. That'll teach me! I signed off. I felt strange—partly sad, partly tired, partly guilty, partly dehydrated, and at the same time somewhat energized, empowered. I didn't have Natalie and I didn't have FancyPants, but 24/7 was back! I was back! Once again anything was possible.

The phone rang.

"Jack here," I answered.

"Jack, it's Pamela," a girl said.

"Pamela . . ."

"Pamela Brown," she said. "You asked me to the prom, remember?"

chapter 25

PAMELA BROWN. HOLY OF HOLIES. Ballet dancer, goddess, the object of my fantasies for three years.

"You may remember," she said, "you tempted me by mentioning cheap cake?"

"Yeah, I remember," I said.

It was odd. I wasn't scared of her. I was too exhausted to try to flirt or be charming or even give a shit. I felt, well, calm.

"I've been thinking," she said, "and I want to kind of turn the tables."

"How's that?"

"Look," she said, "I'm not going to ask you to the prom outright. I know that you've got all kinds of options right now. So all I'm asking for is one date. Just one date. Tomorrow night, Friday. We can talk about the prom then."

The school day on Friday seemed to occupy an entire month. I tried to maintain my morose mood all morning. I wrote the names of all the girls I'd ever had crushes on across the bottom of my shoes. I smooshed my hair around so that I looked like a sleep-deprived prisoner. I unraveled the hem of my T-shirt sleeve.

At lunch Percy concocted all kinds of disasters that could happen on my date. Then he started reminding me of embarrassing moments from my past. It was good to have him back in school.

"I seem to recall," he said, "an incident before the ninth-grade dance. There was, I believe, a spray bottle of perfume that you mistook for breath freshener."

"Shut up," I said.

"Really?" Natalie said. "I never heard that. Jack didn't come to the ninth-grade dance."

Natalie and I hadn't made much eye contact today, and even now she was referring to me in the third person.

Percy pointed at her. "Bingo!"

"Yeah, yeah, yeah," I said.

"After he gargled Gatorade for twenty minutes to try to get rid of the flavor, he got the hiccups . . ." Percy explained.

"I forgot about the Gatorade," I said.

"*Bad* hiccups," Percy said.

"One time I sprayed perfume in my eye," Penelope said.

We all looked at her. She was picking at her sardine sandwich. She always brought unusual sandwiches to school.

"You perfumed your eye?" Percy asked. "What did you think it was, dear? Visine, now in a spray bottle?"

"No, I knew it was perfume. I wanted to force myself to cry, so I thought if I sprayed perfume in my eye, I would."

"Did you?" Natalie said.

"No. But the back of my throat smelled and/or tasted like Chanel for six days."

"I don't even want to know the rest of that story," Percy said. "But I do want to return to our hero, Jack Grammar. I seem to recall how at the first sleepover I went to at his house, he mandated an hour of silent reading before bedtime."

The girls looked at me.

"Well, everyone was being so *loud*," I said. "I just wanted to get some reading done."

Penelope and Percy laughed. Natalie cracked a smile and we looked at each other for a split second. Then Penelope related to us the story of the time she put one of those breath-freshener strips in her eye just to see what it would feel like. Apparently it hurt. We didn't really know what to say to that, so Percy just continued with his stories of my follies.

"Ah," he said, "and then there was the time Jack somehow talked me into seeing if Alessandra Deacon would be interested in going to the fifth-grade square dance with him, and—"

"The square dance!" Penelope screamed. "I forgot about that."

"But there was some confusion," Percy continued, "and Alessandra thought I was asking her to be *my* date. And so we went together."

"There was no confusion," I said, "you just asked her for yourself."

"I deny it," Percy said.

And the anecdotes of the lower points of my life continued, and at some point my self-imposed dark mood just completely disappeared and my heart started beating faster and I started worrying about tonight. This was the old Jack, the less-suave-than-beans Jack.

Natalie and I trailed behind Percy and Penelope as we went back into the school. We didn't say anything to each other until we got to the doors.

Then she said, "Dan came over last night. . . ."

"Did he? And?"

"He said you guys had a talk."

"And?"

"And . . . we even agreed that we were never officially apart."

There were a few minutes before lunch was over, so I went up to the computer lab to check my e-mail. When I got there, I sat down at a computer and brooded. In a way I was glad that Natalie and Dan were back together. I wanted them to be happy, right? But at the same time things still felt so weird with Natalie. And it all sort of stung somehow.

There was an issue of the school paper on the chair next to me. It was the special just-off-the-press "Dateline Prom" edition, with all its direct and indirect coverage of me. It was about twice as big as the normal edition of the paper. There was massive speculation about what was going on with 24/7. Rumor had it that I was bringing a college professor to the prom. Someone suggested that I had no intention of coming to the prom at all and the whole scheme was just a joke, a way for me to humiliate girls. Me, a misanthrope? Me, a misogynist? Celia Proctor, Melanie Frankel, and Dee Whalen all gave long interviews about their time with me. Melanie, for one, raised the possibility that I was gay, or at least asexual. And on the last page there was a special prom episode of *Blatt!*, my favorite cartoon. I'd never gotten a chance to go out with Ada Smith, and she apparently took it as a personal insult because she targeted me in her comic today. The robot-controlled puppets in *Blatt!* found themselves stranded on an island with a leper colony of mimes. Yes, the mime lepers were robot-controlled puppets, too, and the name of the colony was Mimes A-wastin'. And one of the robot-controlled leper mimes was named, suspiciously, Jacques G., and he wore a tuxedo T-shirt, and he was reportedly one of the most famous and sought-after mimes in the world, but he had treated people poorly and therefore fate had given him leprosy and premature balding. And in the strip, as he pushed against the side of the invisible box he was trapped in, his arm fell off. One of the main characters, Princess Pea, thereupon commented, "Too bad he's got another one."

All in all, it seemed pretty cruel.

I signed into my e-mail and there were some e-mails from girls not on the list and there was an e-mail from FancyPants. Part of me didn't want to open it. By getting all tangled up in the Natalie mess, I'd kind of soured on FancyPants, too. But really I was happy to see the e-mail from her. She *did* exist. She was still out there.

Jack—

Wondering how your week is going. Can't you give a girl an update?

I wanted to mention that I heard that Laura Gilden is going to the prom with Chris Daley. They're keeping it secret until the last moment. She hasn't told you, has she? But the bad part is that supposedly in exchange for going out once with you, she got set up with Chris. Does that make any sense to you? I really think you need to be careful here. I think there's something going on behind the scenes that you're not in on. I really hate to sound like a whistle-blower or something, but I thought you had a right to know. Not that you haven't heard a lot of baseless rumors about yourself lately.

FP

Laura Gilden? Going out with me in exchange for being set up with Chris Daley? He certainly was more her type—golden boy, et cetera. He'd been on the baseball team at West High with Dan last year. I had met him a couple of times, but I didn't know him. Anyway, what FancyPants was saying wasn't more troubling than the stupid crap the newspaper was printing or the rumors Penelope kept me posted about. Sarah Shay had been collecting rumors for me, too, and e-mailing them to me. It was very sweet. I liked that FancyPants was trying to help me, but she seemed to be taking it too seriously. These were just rumors.

I didn't respond to FancyPants's e-mail. I would do it later.

I stopped in front of Pamela's house at seven. I double-checked the address I had written down on a Post-it note. This was it. It was on the southeast side of town, just south of Kmart, and it wasn't what I was expecting. It was just a dinky little split-level in a neighborhood near the highway. Even sitting there in the car, I could hear the traffic droning past. The neighborhood was youngish, the trees were small, the lawns were almost uniform— no flowers, no interesting plants. There was a battered bus shelter just up the street. This all seemed surprising. I'd always pictured Pamela living in a cottage surrounded by a meadow of lilies.

As I got out of the car, two big Dobermans barked at me from their chain-link kennel next door. I waved to them. I went up the sidewalk. Pamela's place was clean, for sure. Neat. I was reaching for the doorbell when the door opened and Pamela came out.

"Hi, Jack," she said. And she gave me a peck on the cheek. "Any trouble getting to me?"

"Not at all," I said. Of course, the real answer was, well, it did take me three years before I even got the nerve to ask you out. Then you said yes. Then you said no. Then you called me a week later with a sudden change of heart.

We walked to the car. She was wearing a flapper-type dress. I knew that Natalie thought Pamela looked like an ostrich, but to me she was perfect. Perhaps that just meant I liked ostriches.

I fumbled with the remote key fob, first locking us out of the car, then popping the trunk. Finally I got the door open for her. She got in the car and I shut the door on her purse strap. I opened the door and she reeled her purse strap in.

We drove back to the center of town, talking about what we were going to do this summer.

"Oh, I'll just be working at Barnes and Noble again," I said "Or *still,* I guess."

"Uh-huh," she said nodding.

"I'm a sales associate," I said, as if it were impressive. *Everyone* was a sales associate.

"Cool," she said.

"And I'm drawing up a big summer reading list. Twenty great American novels."

I felt sort of like I was talking to my aunt Vanessa—giving all the proper answers to all the proper questions. Also, it was a complete lie about the list of novels.

"That sounds great," she said. "Very productive."

"I'm pretty productive," I said.

Pamela, as usual, was touring with a ballet company this summer, although she would be home three days a week.

"So, what's it like to tour with a ballet company?" I asked.

"I really like it," she said. "It's great."

"Cool," I said. "That sounds great. Must be fun."

"It is," she said. "I mean, it's hard work, but it's fun at the same time, you know."

"Yeah."

Riveting stuff.

We parked downtown and went to College Street Billiards. She picked a table while I got the balls. It wasn't crowded. Only two other tables were occupied.

I had imagined Pamela playing pool with grace and ease, but I was wrong. When she went to break, she actually missed the balls altogether, something I'd never seen happen. Later she hit the cue ball too low and it jumped off the table. In other words, we were pretty evenly matched. We both sucked, and luck dictated who won. (I did.)

We didn't talk much. I had hoped that the game would loosen us up before dinner, let us get comfortable around each other so we could have a better conversation. But as we walked to the restaurant through the last light of day, I realized that not only was I less relaxed than I'd been at the start of the date, but she was nervous, too. From that forced-casual kiss on the cheek to the scripted dead-end questions in the car to the way we were walking spaced very far apart so we wouldn't accidentally bump into each other . . . I couldn't believe it: Pamela Brown was nervous. I never thought someone like her would be awkward or shy or flustered. But she was. Her speech was clipped, and she would give these airy, fake little nervous laughs in the middle of talking. She was shy about making eye contact. Her shyness played off my shyness in some horrible shyness feedback loop, which just made things more halting and awkward.

We walked north on Linn Street and then turned east. Despite our best efforts, we bumped into each other briefly as we turned the corner but didn't say anything about it—just ignored it. Then across the street I saw Adrian Swift coming out of the video store. And she saw me, too. Or, I should say, she saw *us*. This seemed to happen so often it was almost funny. Almost.

Pamela had made reservations for us at the Motley Cow Café, in the north side neighborhood. My parents loved this place, and I liked it—especially the Fon-Tuesdays in the winter when they served fondue.

The Motley Cow—dubbed by Natalie the Mad Cow—was tiny. Picture your living room. Now halve it. Then you've got the approximate size of the restaurant. There were maybe six tables, and the kitchen was right there at the back and you could see what was going on. Two guys were working away back there tonight as Pamela and I were seated. Pamela read the menu carefully—not that it was a long menu. Pamela and I both ordered salads and panini.

We talked about school and college for a longish while, in the same talking-to-your-relatives fake way. Our salads came. We ate quietly for a little bit. I was sitting up as straight as I could, keeping my elbows off the table.

"You probably think I didn't know who you were," she said out of the blue. "But I did."

"Me? You knew who I was?"

"Remember, I did know your name that day we talked."

That day we talked. *The fantastic transgenic forces of springtime . . .*

"Oh, yeah," I said. It was true. She had known my name. And it was something I didn't understand. I'd puzzled over it.

"Don't you know how I knew you?"

"You said you saw me playing with my dog in the park sometimes."

"Right, but I knew you before that. I recognized you in the park, but I already knew who you were."

"Then I don't know the answer."

"Honestly?" she asked.

"Honestly."

"We were in kindergarten together," she said.

"Kindergarten?"

"Mrs. Egan's morning kindergarten."

"I don't remember you."

"People called me Bea back then. Bea Brown."

"Bea Brown . . ." I said. I pushed my salad plate aside. "Bea Brown."

"Beatrice is my first name."

"Bea Brown . . ." I said again, remembering. Long flaxen hair in two pigtails. White shoes. Purple backpack. "You held my hand," I said.

She nodded. "More than once."

"You declared I was your boyfriend on the very first day."

"It's embarrassing."

"That was you?" I asked.

"That was me."

"You're Bea Brown!" I said. "I remember. But I think I owe you an apology. Back then, I wasn't particularly experienced in the girlfriend department and I think perhaps I didn't reciprocate or even acknowledge you."

"You were a little dense," she said. "When I asked if I could hold your hand on the playground, you asked why."

"Uh-huh," I said. "Clueless. Clueless. That's when all my troubles started."

"You did give me a drawing you had done of some kind of robot."

"A Transformer?"

"And underneath it you wrote my name, though most of the letters were backward."

"See, I did like you. I drew that picture because I liked you. I didn't see the point of the hand-holding, but I think I figured that pictures of Transformers would communicate how I felt."

She laughed. "My mom still remembers me talking about you every day. And you came to my birthday party that year. If you could call it a party since it was just me and you and Reba."

"Oh, yeah," I said.

"Of course, we lived over near your house then."

"On Glendale, that's right."

"Yeah."

"But what happened?" I asked. "Bea Brown!" I looked at her. Her face had always seemed familiar to me—I mean, since I first noticed her or re-noticed her a few years ago. So this explained it. I had known her a long time ago. How perfect was this? This was perfect! This was shaping up to be perfect! This whole messy week was really going to come to a spectacular end as I was reunited with my kindergarten sweetheart! This was the storybook plot twist I had been waiting for for years, for my whole life. Should we just skip prom and throw a huge wedding instead? What would we name our kids? What species of hardwood floors would be in our summerhouse? Would we be coffee people or tea people? Or both?

"Where . . ." I said, grasping for words. I didn't quite know what to say, I was so excited. "Where did you go? How did we lose track of each other?"

"I don't really know," she said. "My family moved across town. We were in different schools than each other until high school."

Our panini came. I wasn't that hungry, but I started eating. I shook my head. "I can't believe it. Bea Brown. I think my parents have a picture of us," I said. "And you remember me, you made the connection, but I didn't."

"It was a long time ago. I looked sort of different."

"Let's see, twelve years ago. Twelve years . . . Wow."

"I liked you a lot."

"I'm embarrassed I didn't make the connection, didn't remember you."

"Don't be."

"But I don't get it. If you knew who I was all along, why did you never say hi? Why'd you think I was a sophomore when we talked last week?"

She shrugged. She was picking at her panini, not eating. "I don't know," she said. "It's just so weird. People move along, their paths cross, then they diverge. Then they cross again years later. I was nervous, I guess. I was just looking for some excuse. I didn't know what other people would think. I don't know."

"What other people would think?" I asked. "Like how?"

"What I mean . . ." she said. "I . . ."

"What *other people* would think?" I repeated. That didn't sound right. That didn't sound good. Hold on a second. Hold on a cotton-picking minute.

"I mean, I wouldn't normally go to these kinds of things—to the prom—and I was nervous all of a sudden."

"That's not what you just said."

"I know." Her voice was small now. "I didn't mean it."

"Bea Brown," I said, "listen to me. What happened in the past week that made you change your mind about going to the prom with me?"

"Don't you see, Jack, that I like you and that I just needed to sort it out for myself? I'm just socially reluctant. I'm unsure. It's a weakness."

"I want you to try to answer my question."

"Jack . . ." she said, and she reached across the table for my hand. I let her touch it. "It's hard to explain."

"Then let me venture a guess," I said. "Please correct me if my assumptions are off. Nutshell: last week I asked you to the prom, you were tempted because you sort of liked me, but then you thought, no, he's basically a dorky nobody, not good enough for me, not cute enough for me, not manly enough for me—even if I was your kindergarten sweetheart, times are different now. This week different story. Suddenly I'm what people are talking about. I'm popular. I'm sought after. I'm it. Lots of girls want to go to the prom with me. I didn't really *do* anything to deserve all this attention, I didn't change, I didn't even buy any new clothes, but that's the reality nonetheless."

She was looking at her plate, still touching my hand.

"In other words," I continued, "you changed your mind not because of some soul-searching on your part or because you realized you made a mistake, but because I've been transformed into some kind of trophy, and you thought, hey, he could be mine. He *was* mine once. People think he's pretty cool, he's pretty great, therefore I think so, too."

"I don't just want a trophy," she said.

"Then tell me right now, in all honesty, that you would want to go to prom with me if it wasn't for the twenty-four/seven thing."

She was quiet. She looked at her food. Finally she spoke again. "It's complicated," she said.

"That's a no." It was. It was a big, big no. It felt like the biggest no I had ever heard.

For the past few minutes it had been like I was riding to the top of the world's tallest skyscraper on a turbo elevator—with that smooth and dizzying sensation of blind ascension in the cradle of my stomach. Going up, up, up . . . But then I had reached the top, and the elevator doors had slid quietly open, and I stepped out into the silence only to find nothing beneath my feet. I was falling, falling fast. Only she could save me now, but only by some miracle. Falling was much faster than ascending, even in a turbo elevator.

"It's complicated," she repeated. She took a sip of water, and I could see that she was scared and for a split second I was angry and disappointed with her, then almost instantly my anger turned to pity. In the same circumstances, wouldn't I have been swayed by the court of public opinion, too? If the dorky fifteen-year-old car you *sort of* like suddenly becomes a hip retro car, is it wrong for you to suddenly love it? If Burt Reynolds goes from being the B-grade has-been to the Oscar-grade star of today, aren't you allowed to like him? When mac and cheese starts showing up on high-class menus, don't you think that's pretty darn cool for the lowly carb and Velveeta mash you used to eat in your pajamas while you watched *X-Files* reruns late at night?

Pamela sniffled. "It was just something in the back of my mind, I admit," she said. "Then Reba talked to Laura Gilden, and

Laura told her how sweet you'd been on your date with her, and then I started thinking about you and wondering if I should have said yes to you, and . . . and . . . I started hearing about you all the time. . . ."

I took a big breath and held it. I let it go. We weren't holding hands anymore. "I'm sorry things evolved between you and me like they have," I said. "I want you to know that it's been a particularly crazy week for me, and it's difficult for me to trust my own sense of judgment and I don't really feel that I have any right to tell you that the way your feelings have changed is wrong. But I don't think we can go to the prom together."

She nodded.

I sat slumped there. I was drained. My panini had two bites taken out of it, that's all. I didn't know what else to say to Pamela. On the one hand, I wanted to comfort her and say that it was okay and that I understood and that we were all just human beings after all and we made mistakes and we were weak and that's why we needed each other in the first place. But on the other hand, I felt cheapened by the situation, and that was impossible to ignore. I kept picturing that moment in the hallway a week ago—it felt like years ago, but it was only a week—that moment when in the space of a few seconds she had gone from being receptive and kind of saying yes to closing herself off to me and turning away. I could feel that that's basically what I was doing right now—turning away. Because I had to.

We sat there waiting for the check, not talking, and my mind had nothing to think about. No amount of thinking or reasoning or problem solving or brainstorming or rationalization or whatever you wanted to call it could salvage the situation. What was it all good for, then? Why be smart if it can't help you out at your lowest moments? I could expound on T. S. Eliot's idea of the objective correlative in *Hamlet,* I could give you a timeline of the events leading up to World War I, I could solve the toughest calculus problems in the book, but I couldn't think my way out of this one.

Then something connected. Maybe Pamela had put me in a suspicious mood. Or maybe it was just the coincidence of Laura Gilden coming up twice in the same day from unexpected quarters—from FancyPants and now from Pamela.

"Hey, I'm just wondering," I said suddenly, "do you know Laura Gilden?"

"Not really. But Reba does." Pamela's friend, tennis partner.

"If it's possible," I said, "can I ask a favor of you? It would mean a lot to me."

"What is it?" she said.

"I need you to have Reba ask Laura Gilden something."

"Okay."

"Tonight, if possible," I said.

"Sure."

"In fact, right now, if possible."

chapter 26

TECHNICALLY I WAS SUPPOSED TO pick my prom date by midnight. Everyone on the list knew that, and as I drove across town to the Country Kitchen, I imagined several of the girls on the list sitting up, waiting by their computers for the e-mail. I knew that not all of them really wanted to go with me—and in light of what I had learned in the past hour and a half, I now wondered if *any* of them did—but surely there were one or two. Callie Cunningham, maybe? Mary Langley-Lola? Who were the ones that truly liked me? That was the question. That was definitely the question.

I was about to get the answer.

I parked and went in and at first I didn't see Natalie or Percy, but then I saw that they were in the far corner. I went over. Bridget was with them.

"We already ordered, buddy," Percy said. "We got you your usual brownie sundae. With coconut."

I shrugged. I looked at Natalie, but she was drawing on her place mat.

"You're welcome," Percy said.

"Thanks," I said. This wasn't going to be easy. I did not want to do this at all.

"I don't even know how you can like coconut," Natalie said, still drawing. "It's a weird nut with water in it."

For some reason, this just made me mad.

"Coconut is almost the best thing on the whole planet," Bridget said, coming to my defense.

"Pshaw," Percy said. "Coconut isn't the best thing on the planet."

"Then what is?" Bridget asked.

"I don't know. Sugar."

"Sugar?" Bridget said. "That's boring."

They probably would have gone on like this all night if I hadn't sighed. They looked at me. Percy kicked me under the table. "So, who's the lucky girl?" he said. "It's Pamela, isn't it? You're holding it all in, but in about three seconds you're going to burst. Now do it! Burst! Tell us!"

"No," I said. "Nope."

"Hey, what's the point of calling an emergency meeting and then not spilling the details? That's not fair."

"It's not fair?" I said. "Not fair?"

"Plus why'd you want Natalie to drag Bridget here past her bedtime?"

"I wanted to have one person here who was my friend," I said. "One friend."

"Ouch, Jack," Percy said. "That hurts. After all I've done for you . . ."

He was jokey. He didn't see what was coming.

"Yeah," Natalie said, "and why are you kind of repeating your-self twice whenever you say something?"

"Am I?" I said. "I am."

"See!" Natalie said. "You just did it again."

"Hey," Percy said, "what do you mean 'repeating yourself twice'? Doesn't repeating *mean* twice?"

"Kiss my brass," Natalie said.

"So wouldn't 'repeating twice' mean saying something three times? Or four?" Percy said.

"Blow it out your porthole," Natalie replied.

"I'm just asking," Percy said.

"Shut up!" I said. "Okay? I'll tell you about Pamela."

That seemed to be a good way to ease into it. I told them everything about my date, and they listened closely and then cursed her appropriately when the big letdown came. The elimination of Pamela, of course, led them to ask me which girl from the list was my escort for tomorrow.

"I don't know yet. I can only go with someone who *wants* to go with me. Maybe no one."

"Maybe no one?" Natalie said. "What are you talking about?"

"I may have to turn them all down."

"Aw, Jack-o," Percy said, "everyone's going to hate you if you don't pick someone."

"And it's against the rules!" Natalie said.

"No, it's not," I said. "And if it is, I don't care."

"I think you should do whatever you feel is right," Bridget said.

"Pipe down," Natalie said. Then she looked at me. "You've wussed out. You've pulled a typical Jack move and just turned away from the challenging stuff."

"Whoa!" I said. After what she'd put me through—put us through—she was accusing me of wussing out? I slapped my hand on the table. "What do you think you're proving by being such a bitch?" I said.

They all stared at me. Natalie's eyes were locked on mine for a moment. Then she went back to her drawing.

"Hey, hey . . ." Percy said. "Calm down."

"If this were a tough school assignment," Natalie said, doodling, "you would have gritted your teeth and done it right and gotten an A, but because it's a social challenge, you flaked out."

"Do I have to remind you both that this all started as a late-night *joke* and that you guys didn't put any thought into it at all?"

"I'm just disappointed is all," Natalie said. "I thought you were going to learn something this week."

"That's bullshit," I said. "I learned a lot this week. A lot. More than I wanted to know about you, for example. And I don't deserve this kind of blame. I didn't flake out. I went on the dates, I did it all. I held up my end of the deal, even though it was a crappy deal. But I was let down. I was let down by you guys."

Percy and Natalie had a blank look. They still didn't get it.

"I know what you guys did," I said. "I know you rigged everything. I know."

"What are you talking about?" Natalie said.

"Did you or did you not get Laura Gilden to agree to go out with me only after you and Dan arranged for her to go out with Chris Daley?"

"Oh," Percy said.

"Well?" I said.

"Yeah," Percy said, "but it wasn't like—"

"Okay, and did you or did you not tell Celia Proctor that I was dying and that I only had a short time to live and that's the only reason she agreed to go out with me?"

Pause.

"And did you or did you not," I continued, "tell Julie Vanderwoude that I was going to be on a reality television show and that the producers were secretly filming my week of dating in order to pick some of the girls to be on the actual show?"

These were the facts I had verified tonight. Pamela's friend Reba had gotten Laura Gilden to tell the truth. I had called Julie myself and asked what the story was. The Celia Proctor thing was thanks to FancyPants, of course, though I hadn't really believed it until tonight. I'd tried to call some of the other girls on the list but hadn't had much luck reaching them.

"And there's more, isn't there?" I said. "Do you care to give me the whole story or not?"

"We were just trying to help you out," Natalie said.

"Help me out! Help me out! Oh, I see, but by 'helping me out' you mean lying to me and misleading me and making me out to be a fool and telling people things that aren't true about me. That's real helpful. That's super-helpful. You should get a Nobel Prize for Helpfulness. Heck, I'll nominate you myself!"

They were quiet. Natalie was biting her lip and Percy was playing with his straw. Only Bridget would look at me.

"Maybe it's just me," I said after a little bit. "Maybe I just misunderstood the meaning of the word 'friend' all these years. Maybe 'friend' actually means a deceitful meddler, not a loyal and well-meaning pal. Maybe I should check into that. It's probably all my fault. My fault. My bad. Sorry. So sorry. I'll just be on my way."

"You're right," Percy said. "We screwed up."

"I mean, I really *love* it when girls pretend to like me out of pity," I said. "How did you guys know that I would *love* that, that it's exactly what I love?"

"We didn't mean to hurt you or to hurt anybody," Natalie said. And it was like she was talking about two things at once: both the deceits she and Percy had pulled and also what had happened between her and me. It was like it was all coming out in the open at once, even though Percy and Bridget didn't know. "But I mean, we put that silly ad online and then we thought, hey, maybe this will actually work, and then it kind of evolved from there. It wasn't some kind of diabolical plan. It evolved, you know."

Evolved. I didn't like that word. It reminded me of Pamela and how her feelings for me had evolved. . . .

"Let's see," I said, "isn't the whole point of evolution that you end up with something better than what came before? How was your plan an improvement over what would have happened?"

"Because look at you, Jack!" Natalie said. "Look at the week you've had. Look at what you've learned and look at what you've done. And look at you right now. You're stronger than you were before and you aren't petrified to talk to a girl and you aren't going to become a recluse next year in college. Now, I know that's not justification for anything we did, but it's a good thing."

"Humor me," I said. "Tell me what happened."

They did. They started talking. Bridget and I just listened. Yes, the original ad was a joke. But then they thought it might actually get me a date for the prom if they made it into a little game.

"How many responses did you get to the ad?" I asked.

"When?" Percy asked.

"Well, on Sunday you told me there were a hundred and forty-nine responses. How many did you have at that point? I mean, how many *real* responses?"

They looked at each other.

"Four?" Percy said.

"Three?" Natalie said. "Something like that."

I dropped my head onto the table. It was worse than I thought.

"So," I said, head down, "you told me there were a hundred and forty-nine to get me pumped up."

"Basically," Natalie said. "We didn't really plan on that number. It just came out. We thought it would get you excited about the scheme. We thought it might be the only way to get you to participate."

"You had three or four responses, and so you two went to work arranging for girls to be on the list by whatever means possible."

"We didn't tell them all lies," Natalie said. "When I asked Callie Cunningham, she knew immediately who you were. She said she would love to go out with you."

"So she doesn't think I'm dying." I was still talking to the tabletop.

"No."

"Or that I'm going to be on TV."

"No."

"Or that I'm, I don't know, a billionaire or something."

"We only told that to a couple of girls," Natalie said.

I looked up. I had been joking. I didn't know they'd told anyone that. "You told someone I was rich?"

"Yeah."

"Who?"

"Laura Schiller."

Cripes. The basketball player I'd been beaten so soundly by.

"Why would anyone believe a lie like that?" I asked.

"Because we're good liars," Natalie said.

"Apparently."

So. To set the record straight, we worked through the whole list. The original four respondents to the ad were Melanie Frankel, aka the girl who jumped off the roof and then took my Goldfish; the CK half of the two girls who wrote JACK on their breasts; Kaylee Pritchett; and Felicia Deatsch, whom they had "weeded out" because they knew I didn't like her.

That was it. Those were the four wonderful girls who actually thought the ad was pretty cool and responded that weekend.

Callie and Sarah went out with me basically just because Natalie asked them to. Laura Gilden—who had gotten me drunk at the country club—went with me in exchange for being introduced to Chris Daley, who was a friend of Dan's. Yes, Julie was told I was going to be on television. Dee Whalen—the religious girl who I had a speed date with at Hetta's house—was Dan's cousin and had gone out with me in exchange for him installing her car stereo. Celia thought I was dying, as did Chance McNamee and a few of the girls I didn't actually go out with. Others fell for the millionaire story.

After Percy and Natalie came clean—and by this point our food had come and gone—I sat in a stupor. I didn't know what to say.

"That's all," Natalie said. "Those are all the lies, I swear."

"All of them, really?" I asked, looking right at her.

She returned my stare.

"But that's not everyone," I said. "There are still a few girls on the list you haven't covered."

"That's the part of the story we've been trying to tell you," Percy said, "but you won't let me. After a couple of days, after word spread around, we started getting all kinds of responses to the ad."

"They liked me because I was famous," I said.

"Some, I guess. But a lot of them were completely genuine. We put some of the better ones right onto the list, like . . ."

"Like Adrian Swift," Natalie supplied.

Poor Adrian, who'd seen me with three different girls. I wished I hadn't lied to her about having rickets last year or about having already chosen someone to go to the prom with. I didn't deserve someone as nice as her. I wondered: did she hit me in the head with her locker on purpose that day? 'Cause she should have.

"Adrian? Who else?"

"Samantha Milligan."

"That freshman?"

"Yeah, isn't she precious?" Natalie said.

"Way too young."

"Let's see," Natalie continued, "also Bess Eberlee, Mary Langley-Lola, Jenny Wester . . . "

I looked at Bridget. She'd just been listening the whole time, but you could tell she'd been thinking everything through. "What do you think I should do?" I asked. "Should I pick someone, or not go to the prom, or what? Should I hire some new friends, at least?"

"I think you have to answer all that for yourself," she said. "This is your life and not anyone else's."

I smiled. "Thank you," I said. "Yay for Bridget."

Back at home, in my room, with the lights out, the door shut, Flip scratching at the door from the hallway, I sat by the window with my legs up on the desk, my arms crossed on my chest. I had about half an hour to notify everyone on the list what my decision was.

Six hours ago I would have chosen Pamela. Two days ago I would have chosen Natalie. Before that, I would have wanted to go with FancyPants. Those girls weren't options anymore. And the list of twenty-four—which had once seemed large and full of potential—had been whittled down in the past few hours. I was not, obviously, going to go to the prom with someone who was only doing it because they thought I was rich or something.

So who was left?

I thought of Callie Cunningham—the long car ride, her dropping that girl's fly ball on purpose. Even now it made me smile. And I remembered Sarah Shay's illegal firework and the sound of our feet and laughter as we ran away from the crime. I'd been a little shy around her, and she'd been shy, too. But I liked it.

And I liked Callie's pet stories and Mary Langley-Lola's song. And her tote bag with that happy whale on it. I wished I had gone out with her. And when Sarah Shay and I had been standing in the fossil gorge, surrounded by the shrill calls of all the peep frogs, I remembered how she lit up when she started talking about the glaciers, the ancient river, the bedrock, the flood. . . .

The dashboard light had lit Callie's face. And when I'd hit my head on Adrian's locker, she knelt down right next to me and she had this look on her face, this look of concern that was so pure that it made me ache. Adrian! Why did I have to screw things up with her? It was just stupid. I'd gone to watch her in the Knowledge Bowl matches last year. One of the questions was what was the meteorological name for rain that evaporates before it reaches the ground. There was a pause—no one seemed to know the answer—and then Adrian buzzed in and said, "Virga." She was right, and I thought it was a marvelous piece of information to know. Rain that evaporates before it reaches the ground . . .

I turned on my computer and waited for it to boot up. I went and opened my door and Flip was asleep on the hallway carpet. I lifted him and brought him into the room and put him on his little doggie bed. After I set him down, he woke up and looked around. He looked up at me and he sighed through his muzzle and then he went right back to sleep. I looked at the computer screen.

I was getting loopy. It was late. How was I supposed to pick one girl? How was I supposed to rank them? I mean, they were people, not television shows or CDs or soft drinks. I'd only spent a few hours with Sarah and Callie and hardly any time with Mary or Adrian. And the fantasy of FancyPants or the near thing of Natalie kept crowding my mind. And Pamela! I still wondered about Pamela. Perhaps I hadn't let her explain herself well enough. Perhaps her sin was a minor one, one to be forgiven.

It was too much. It wasn't sorting itself out. It was a quagmire. I liked these girls I was thinking about, but to pick one was just too reductive. There was something I liked in each one of them, some essence, some detail. . . . The whole 24/7 scheme had been flawed in that it was too artificial a setup. At least for me.

Perkins County Schools
Media Center

I was running out of time, I was running out of energy. 24/7 was over.

So I made my decision. I would choose no one. That was my own decision. That was my final comment on 24/7.

Is rain that evaporates before it reaches earth rain? Yes, but it has its own special name: virga. And is a guy who goes to the prom solo really a guy at all? Yes, but he has his own special name: Jack Grammar.

I wrote the e-mails, I sent them, I sighed.

Before I shut down, I checked to see if FancyPants was online. But I knew she wouldn't be. She wouldn't be up this late. I wrote her a short e-mail:

> Well, let me just say that I adore you, FancyPants, and that I always will.

It had been a night of revelations, and a final one had slipped in there quite unexpectedly. It had come to me suddenly and simply: I knew who FancyPants was. Though she wasn't an option as a prom date, my discovery of her identity didn't make me feel like I'd lost her. Sure, I had lost the dream of FancyPants—the fantasy that she was my soul mate and that sooner or later we would meet and spend all eternity together. But instead of a dream, now there was a real person. And that wasn't bad at all. That was a good thing.

I did adore her, and I would talk to her tomorrow.

chapter 27

NATALIE WOKE ME UP with a phone call. I knew it was her. No one else would call me that early on a Saturday.

"Spill the beans," she said. She didn't even say hello.

"I've got no beans. No beans here."

"Don't annoy me!"

"Annoy you? You're the one that woke me up."

"Be like that," she said. "I'm too busy anyway. I guess I'll just find out who your date is when me and Dan come to pick you up."

"There will be nothing to see, I'm afraid."

The line was silent. "Okay, tell me that you're going with someone. Tell me you picked *someone*."

"On the contrary, madam, I picked no one. Everyone on the list remains unpicked. There was no wild-card surprise. There was no about-face on Pamela. I am going to my own prom unattached."

"It's your decision," she said dismissively.

"And I feel great about it!" I said. "I feel really good. So ha."

"Okay, Jack," she said. "Very impressive. I'll catch you later."

And I did feel good. Why? Well, why question it? Maybe it was just a normal Saturday high. Maybe it was that I enjoyed yelling at Natalie. Maybe it was the fact that for the first time in a week, I wouldn't be stressed out about a date (or dates) tonight. I would go to the prom, I would dance, I would walk around unattached, I would tell witty stories to underclassmen, I would smile, I would flirt with the female teachers, I would be everywhere and do everything and see everyone. It was my prom. *My* prom. I was going to look great and I was going to feel great and what was the point of a pity party anyway? I *could* have gone with someone. There were certainly several girls on the list who actually wanted to go with me, and then there were plenty of girls who weren't on the list who liked me, too. I *could* have gone with someone. Maybe next week I would call up Sarah or Callie or Mary and we'd plan a date. Maybe. We would choose a pace that was comfortable. But tonight it was just me.

It was a strange sensation. Here I was, about to go to my own prom alone and I was completely at ease with that. I felt unfettered. I was light on my feet. What last week had been my greatest fear—going to the prom alone—was now my preference.

I went running, and the morning air was pleasantly cool and the streets were quiet. Lo and behold, there was Lucy, my Firefly Club companion, running toward me by the river.

"Jack," she called, smiling.

"Lucy." I smiled back.

We joined up and ran together.

She talked about her hectic semester and how she was going to job interviews in Chicago and Houston and Sacramento next week and how she was trying to finish up her classes and arrange for her family to come for graduation and moving in with her boyfriend and how she'd just had her car rear-ended by some grad-student poet type in a little SUV and how the poet's insurance was being slow about a settlement while Lucy drove around town with her rear bumper attached to her car with duct tape.

"So what's your week been like?" Lucy asked.

Heck. My prom worries didn't seem like much of anything compared to the stuff Lucy was talking about.

"Prom's tonight," I said.

"Oh, yeah?"

"Yep. And I'm going by myself."

"Bravo," she said. "So you're flying solo. I'll tell you a secret. I went to my senior prom by myself."

"But you're a righteous babe."

"I know," she said. "Obviously. But there was just no one I really, really wanted to go with. So I didn't."

"That makes sense," I said. "I like that."

"And have you started reading *Watership Down* yet?"

"The thing about that," I said, "is that I have no plans to read it. It just kind of slipped out of my mouth when we were talking last week."

"I hear you," she said. "It is a good book, though. After you mentioned it last weekend, I started reading it. I'm halfway through."

"It's really good? Then I'll read it this summer."

"You seem different today," she said, out of the blue.

"Like how?"

"Like you don't seem like you're hiding from the world. Does that make sense?"

"It does," I said. And I nodded while we ran.

Percy's brother had Percy's car, and Penelope and Natalie both had two-hour hair appointments at Groovy Katz, so Percy called me before noon and asked for a ride to the hospital. I was about to leave for work anyway, so I drove him over there and on the way he asked me to come up and see Mr. K.—who was much improved. If Mr. K. remained stable, he would have bypass surgery Monday.

"He's been very entertained by my stories about your week of girls," Percy told me as we turned into the parking garage, "and I know he'd love to see you."

"That's great," I said. "Using my foibles as anecdotes for everyone's amusement."

"He's not just anyone. I figured anything that made him laugh was good for him."

When he put it that way, I didn't mind. I had a little time before I needed to be at work, so we parked and went into the hospital. I was glad Percy knew his way around because we walked a long way through various wings and pavilions. Even though it was a Saturday, the hospital was busy, and the cafeteria was packed as we passed. One of the central atriums was sunny and full of plants and a guy was playing piano there.

When we got to Mr. K.'s room, I hung a bit behind Percy. It was dim in the room, and the TV was on. I couldn't tell if Mr. K. was asleep or awake. He was slumped down in the bed. The other bed in the room was empty.

Percy went straight to the window blinds and opened them up, brightening the room. Mr. K. jerked.

"I'm awake!" he said. "You didn't catch me asleep! No!"

"I know, I know . . ." Percy said. "Look, I brought Jack."

"Hey, Mr. K.," I said, waving. "It's good to see you."

"Mr. Jack!" he said. He stuck out his hand. I shook it. "I've been hearing about all your escapades and that. You're some kind of guy."

"That's what they tell me," I said.

"You must be a good dancer," he said. "Percy told me you took dance lessons for your sister's wedding and that you cut a fine figure on the dance floor."

"I get by," I said.

"You gotta keep all those girls busy," he said. "Ha!"

"Who's here?" someone said behind me. It was Mrs. Kowalski, entering.

"Look, it's Mr. Jack," Mr. K. said.

"Oh, now, it's so nice you came up," she said. "We've been hearing about all your escapades and that."

"That's what Mr. K. said," I said.

"You must be a good dancer," she said.

"I just covered that with him," Mr. K. said. "He's a great dancer. Keeps all those girls busy. Ha!"

"So which one's going to be your date tonight?" Mrs. Kowalski asked. "We heard that you liked Sarah. You know, she's Penelope's friend, and we adore Penelope."

I told them that Sarah was great but that I'd decided to go to the prom alone.

"Alone!" Mrs. Kowalski exclaimed. "That's just not right. You should pick someone. Don't tease the girls like that!"

"That's what me and Natalie told him," Percy said.

"But look," Mr. K. said, "if he goes alone, he can dance with more girls. Dance with everyone! Ha! He's a smart one, Mr. Jack."

Mr. K. asked me to sit right by his bedside. I needed to go, but I decided it wouldn't hurt if I was ten minutes late. Then Mr. and Mrs. K. started telling me about all the proms they'd been to over the years.

"We just really love seeing all the kids," Mrs. K. said. "And they're all so nice to us."

"And the dancing! We love the dancing," Mr. K. added.

"Dancing?" Percy said to his grandfather. "You always grumble about the dancing."

"I'm the one that likes the dancing!" Mrs. K. said.

"And that's why *I* like it," Mr. K. said, winking at me. "Because it makes her happy."

Mrs. K. smiled at him.

"And she loves being out late!" Mr. K. said.

"Like how late?" I asked.

"Oh," Mrs. K. said, "ten thirty."

I nodded.

"One time, eleven!" Mrs. K. said.

"Now, of course, this year," Mr. K. said, "the docs say I can't go."

"Leave it to doctors to deny you something enjoyable," I said.

"I mean, I feel fit to fly, but they just won't let me out of this joint."

"Fascist so-and-so doctors," I said.

"We've been doing the opening dance for years," Mrs. K. said. "And we're going to miss it."

Mr. K. looked at me silently for a moment. Then he pointed at me. Then the pointing moved closer and it became a poking—he was poking my chest.

"Since we can't go," he said, "you have to enjoy it for us. And you and Percy and Penelope and Natalie have to tell us all about it."

"It's a deal," I said.

chapter **28**

FELICIA DEATSCH CAME OVER AND talked to me on her break. I was shelving some new books.

"Hi, Felicia," I said.

"Hi," she said. She sat down right in the aisle. She seemed a little glum.

I didn't know what to say. She'd wanted to be on the list but had been cut first thing by Percy and Natalie.

"Well," she said, "the word's out that you didn't choose anyone."

"That's right," I said, still shelving books.

"Seems like kind of a waste," she said.

"I don't know."

She stood up but lingered. I looked up from my work. Her eyes were brimming with tears.

"But I didn't even make the list," she said. "So I don't know why it even matters to me."

This was great. This was what I needed: Felicia Deatsch crying.

"You know I didn't choose the list," I said, but it seemed little comfort to her.

"I've got a dress," she said. "I don't know what to do with it."

"You should wear it to the prom," I said. "That's what you should do with it."

"Yeah . . ." she said, wiping her tears on her cuff. "No one asked me last year. And no one asked me this year."

"Come to think of it," I said, "no one really actually asked me, either. Not directly."

"That's different," she said.

"Anyway, *I'm* going by myself," I said. "Promise me I'll see you there."

She nodded.

"Promise me one dance."

She nodded again.

"One dance *minimum*," I said.

She smiled.

When I checked my phone during my break, it showed that someone had called three times without leaving a message. But I didn't recognize the number. It was a local number, but it had no name with it. Who was it? Someone from the list? Was I going to start getting harassed by the girls I'd turned down?

I walked out of the store into the parking lot, holding my phone, looking at the strange local number. I put the phone in my pocket and started to walk the perimeter of the parking lot— something I did on my break when I tired of being indoors. It was a nice sunny, May day outside, and I felt very alive, even after having worked all afternoon.

My phone rang. It was that same unidentified number.

"Hello?"

"Jack? You sound weird." It was Percy.

"Hey, what number are you calling from?"

"I'm still at the hospital, bud."

"Oh. I should have figured that one out."

"I wouldn't have bothered you at work, but Lloyd's still got my car."

"Where the heck is he?"

"No idea."

"Well, we were counting on your car for our transportation tonight."

"I know, I know."

"And my parents need the Camry . . ."

"We'll all cram into Dan's Camaro."

"Five of us? Oh, I guess that'll work."

"Just means you can't bring any last-minute dates."

"Don't worry about *that*," I said.

"You know what I think," Percy said. "I think you fell in love with yourself this week. That's why you don't want to go with anyone."

"Interesting theory," I said. "And you know what? I do sort of feel like I'm in love, but the funny thing is I'm not in love with anyone."

"But yourself."

"My haircut *is* pretty cool."

At the hospital I parked in the same garage I'd parked in this morning. I wasn't totally sure how to get to Mr. K.'s room from the front entrance, but I knew the way by going through the cafeteria. I found Percy there, carrying a paper plate.

"Percy!" I called.

He clapped me on the back. "Hey, amigo."

"What are you eating?"

"Meat loaf. Peas."

"But we're going out to dinner in a few hours."

"Don't you worry about my appetite."

"If you want to ruin your prom dinner, fine," I said.

"Good," he said. "Hey, you know who's in love with you, man? My grandparents. They've talked about you ever since you left. They kept trying to remember every sentence you said verbatim."

"Why?"

"Beats me. I think *they* would ask you to the prom if they could."

I stood watching him finish off his meat loaf in the middle of the hallway. There was a lot of foot traffic moving around us. Suddenly I had an idea.

"Are they still here?" I asked.

"Who?" Percy said.

"Your grandparents."

"You think Gramps just wandered out of the hospital or something?"

"No, I . . ."

"What?" he said. He could tell something was up.

"I got this idea."

"Uh-oh," he said.

"I want to ask them something."

part **4**

chapter **29**

MOM AND DAD TOOK PICTURES of me in the parlor, in the kitchen, in my room, on the staircase, in the doorway, on the porch, in front of the flower beds, on the deck, by the garden, on the lawn, under the redbud tree, by the birdbath, at the curb, hanging from a low branch, doing a karate kick, throwing a stick for Flip, kissing Flip, chasing Flip, and holding my hand in front of the camera lenses.

"Work it, work it!" Dad said as I did some fake model poses. "You're a rock star!"

Mom was taking pictures with the Nikon and the little point-and-shoot. Dad was fumbling around with the digital camera. Mom reloaded the Nikon with more film. She had started with five rolls at her disposal. Dad fretted with the digital camera.

"Oops," he said.

"Why 'oops'?" Mom asked, still reloading her film.

"I think I just erased everything," Dad said. We both looked at him, and he grimaced and handed the camera over to me. Indeed, the screen was blank.

"Yeah," I said. "Uh-huh. The problem here is that you turned the camera off." I turned it back on and the pictures were all there.

"Who knew?" Dad said.

"Okay, buster," Mom said to me, "how about some pictures against the oak tree?"

"All this for a boy in a tuxedo?" I said. I had complained through the entire photo session but not too loudly because I liked the attention and they were both being sweet and the tuxedo felt great. My date was going to swoon. That's right, my date.

We were just starting a round of photos *without* my tuxedo jacket on when Dan and Natalie rumbled up in Dan's stepfather's '69 Camaro. My parents greeted them loudly and Dan shook Dad's hand and Natalie and my mom hugged and then Dan slapped me on the back and grinned and Natalie said a very quiet, "Hi." Their arrival, of course, initiated a whole new flurry of photography—Nat and Dan on the porch, Nat and Dan kissing, Nat and Dan and me with arms linked, Nat leaning alluringly against the Camaro, Nat carried aloft by me and Dan, and so forth. The car itself merited some photographs and Dad couldn't stop whistling at it. And Natalie in her black vintage dress was beautiful and poised. Dan looked slightly apish in his tux, and for some inexplicable reason he was wearing flip-flops instead of shoes, but as usual he was making everybody feel good and when finally, citing the hour, we three begged our leave and absconded mirthfully within the azure Camaro (with white racing stripes), he let me drive.

As we started the drive across town, I didn't know what to say—I felt a little awkward being in the car with Natalie and Dan, and I wondered how much Natalie had told Dan about what had happened between Natalie and me. But the evening was fair and the air was like velvet and I relaxed. I drove slowly to savor the journey, and Natalie kept sighing and smiling and extending her arm out the window. Even Dan was quiet, which was unusual, and I could see him smiling in the rearview mirror.

We stopped at the curb in front of Percy's house and all got out. I asked Nat and Dan to wait just a minute, and I walked up the sidewalk myself and rang the doorbell with purpose and dignity.

Penelope opened the door almost immediately.

"Hi, Jack!" she said. "You look great! You look good enough to lick!"

After returning the compliment—her salmon-colored dress was surprisingly refined—I explained to her that perhaps she could oblige me by letting me ring the bell again—and not answering it herself this time. She understood and said of course that would be the right thing to do, so she closed the door and I waited a sensible fifteen seconds. I looked back at Natalie and Dan, who were nuzzling each other by the trunk of the car, and then I rang the bell again.

Percy answered, chewing something.

"What are you eating?" I asked.

He held up a banana. Then he said, "Hold on a second, bro. I don't think she knows you're here."

I stopped him, though, and explained what I wanted to happen and he understood and he closed the door and this time I waited thirty seconds, rang again, and this time the right person answered. My date, Mrs. Kowalski.

She inhaled audibly when she saw me and I smiled evenly and gently at her.

"Good evening, Mrs. Kowalski," I said. "May I be so bold as

to say that you look radiant and your dress is a thing of sparkling beauty?"

"Yes, you may, Jack."

"In that case: you look radiant and your dress is a thing of sparkling beauty."

She laughed and I presented her with the corsage. I pinned it on her and Penelope caught the moment on video and then we all gathered in the front yard for more pictures. The next-door neighbor—Mrs. Dunkin, wearing a bathrobe—took a few group photos of us and then the standing-around-not-quite-going-any-where-yet part of the evening was over and I pulled the keys out of my pocket—the keys Mr. K. had given me only a few hours ago—and Percy and I went around back and got in Mr. K.'s white Cadillac—which happened to be from 1986, the year of my birth—and drove it slowly around the side of the house and parked in the driveway so that we could load up. When I'd asked Mr. and Mrs. K. if she would be my date for the evening, they had agreed under two conditions: I had to have her home by eleven, and I had to drive Mr. K.'s Caddy. That, I had assured them, would not be a problem.

We followed Natalie and Dan across town—Mrs. K. in the front seat with me, Percy and Penelope in back—then parked at the hospital and went up to see Mr. K. Here there were more pictures and some jokes about me making a play for Mrs. Kowalski while Mr. Kowalski was still slightly alive. The nurses asked us to parade past the nursing station, and they clapped as we did so and then we all piled into the elevator with one confused-looking resident and the doors closed and the elevator slowly descended and Mrs. Kowalski hiccuped. Percy turned to the resident.

"Excuse me," Percy said, "but we're looking for the psychiatric ward."

Then it was on to dinner downtown. There was no parking near the restaurant, so we parked at the Sheraton parking garage and paraded through the downtown pedestrian mall. Natalie and Penelope walked out in front of us, arms linked, belting a Garth Brooks song that Penelope liked.

"Look at them," Percy said to me. "They're loony."

Someone was hooting or yelling in the near distance, but we all ignored it. It turned out to be a college kid who had seen Mrs. K.'s corsage fall off and had tried to alert us to it but finally just picked it up and ran after us to return it. We thanked him and then I pinned it to Mrs. K. for the second time that evening, and we crossed Washington Street and were honked at by the cars at the stoplight and we waved and Percy blew kisses to them—which immediately silenced the honking—and we ambled casually into the restaurant, which was warm, fragrant, and already crowded with promgoers like us. Our table was waiting for us, though, and after we sat down, we made an immediate toast to Mr. K.—may he speed his way back to health—and then Percy started eating bread from the bread basket.

When we emerged from the restaurant, stuffed and glowing, the velvet air of the early evening had become the silken air of early night, and now there was a hint of moisture in the atmosphere and a nearly full moon was rising at the east end of Washington Street—which was exactly where we were headed.

Through some stroke of genius, madness, or sheer stupidity—or any combination of the three—the prom committee this year had envisioned and somehow pulled off the first outdoor prom in

City High's history. Their arguments that it would be much cheaper than booking a ballroom somewhere (and that the savings would be returned to the school) were persuasive, and soon the administration and parents and kids and town were all rallying around the idea. The football field/track was the location—behind the school. In the event of rain we'd probably have to move into the gym, but no one really gave that part much thought. And through some miracle of lobbying and ass kissing and behind-the-scenes parental manipulations, First Avenue—the street that ran right by the football field—was closed to all traffic for the night. All traffic except prom traffic.

So we drove up First Avenue, in a long line of kid-filled cars, and when we got to the gate that led to the track, we got out and handed over the keys to the valet parking service. (Yes, valet parking, which had been a big selling point of the outdoor prom plan.) Before us was a broad red carpet leading into the prom—into Xanadu, to be specific—and a series of arches made out of ropes of balloons. We waited for Dan and Natalie. A lot of people were clustered around here, waiting for friends, watching the people enter, snapping photos.

"This is prom?" I said, standing there in the crowd. All in all, it felt like a crowded movie theater lobby except that everyone was dressed up.

"Not yet, schlomoe," Penelope said. Then Dan and Natalie walked up and we all nodded and started walking in.

The lights on the carpet were bright, the crowd was thinner, and everyone was headed the same way. It was a river of promgoers.

"It's Jack Grammar and his date!" someone called nearby, and before I knew it, there were two photographers scurrying along in front of me, trying to get a snapshot of my entrance with Mrs. K.

There was the yearbook photographer and the school newspaper photographer. That was all.

"Where's *The New York Times*?" I said. "Where's *People* magazine?"

As we moved down the curving red carpet, beneath the huge balloon hoops, the lighting slowly grew dimmer, and the rush and jumble of the evening suddenly faded away in my mind and I sensed we were in a transition. I could feel my heartbeat and I felt like I was about to step onstage in the most famous theater in the world. Not that it was all about me—and not that I was the lead actor—but it was about all of us, and there was no turning back and there was no hiding and that was just fine by me. But there wasn't, after all, any script, and I was nervous. But in a good way.

By the time we reached the end of the carpet, everything was dance-club dim. We could see the dance floor now—the broad expanse of empty blond wood in the middle of the football field—but there were no dancers. It wasn't time yet. There were several open-sided tents set up in the infield, and the lights inside them made their violet roofs glow. To the left of the track were the lights and sounds of some kiddie carnival rides. There was a breeze in our faces, and it smelled of freshly cut grass and popcorn. Above the dance floor was a net of blue Christmas lights.

We stood in line near the end of the carpet. We checked in at a table and then were put into a short line that ended with the drama teacher, Mr. Tangier. Perched on a stool, with his long tuxedo tails hanging down, he was announcing the name of each arrival over the public address system. We were just moments away from entering now, and I couldn't stop smiling. My fingers were tingling.

Penelope kissed me quickly on the cheek.

"See you on the other side," she said.

Percy and Penelope were announced and they went in and their forms faded into darkness.

Then Dan and Natalie entered.

"Oh, it's all so magical," Mrs. K. said.

Then we were announced:

"Presenting Mr. Jack Grammar and Mrs. Elanora Kowalski."

We stepped forward.

chapter **30**

THERE WAS A SURREAL MOMENT in the middle of the first dance, as Mrs. K. and I glided across the empty floor with the spotlight on us and everybody crowded around watching, when I didn't feel like I was in my body. I was above my body, hovering there, and my body was doing a smooth and excellent job of dancing, and my body was happy and full of life and I was there just above it, looking, watching, taking it in. I could see myself smiling. I could see Mrs. K. smiling. But I couldn't hear the music, and I couldn't smell anything or feel Mrs. K.'s hands or feel my own body, for that matter.

And as I watched us dance, I thought, I wonder what the prom is going to be like? Will it be boring? Will I dance? Will I hover around the margins? Or will it be surprising? Will it be wonderful? Will it be like anything I've ever done? Will it be a dream or a reality? Then I wondered: What is the dinner before the prom going to be like? What will I eat? Will I have an appetite? What should I order? And who, after all, am I going to take to the prom? What exactly will I wear? And who will drive?

I thought how interesting it was going to be to discover the answers to all these questions—and the hundreds more that I had been wondering about for days, weeks, years. But then, of course, I sort of snapped back to reality. It was kind of like the jerk you feel when the roller coaster starts, and suddenly I was back in my body, still dancing, still happy, still smiling, and I realized that many of those questions had already been answered. *I was at the prom. I was at my prom.* What I'd dreamed and wondered about for so long was no longer in the future. Part of it was already in the past, part of it was still in the future, and part of it, of course, was right here, right now, happening. It was happening, and that was just fine. That was, in fact, quite lovely. I wanted to be exactly where I was at the moment, and in a way that was a new feeling for me.

After the first song ended, I bowed to Mrs. K. I didn't plan that, I just did it. She patted my hand and the crowd clapped and the deejay said something and then suddenly the next song started and the students rushed onto the dance floor and instead of being alone with Mrs. K., I was now surrounded by everyone.

I danced with Penelope. I danced with Sarah Shay. Then I danced with Mrs. K. again, then Penelope again, then two girls I didn't know. I danced two songs in a row with Felicia Deatsch, and she had this weird but hilarious way of dancing where she kept tossing up the hem of her dress. She knew she was being funny. She was doing it on purpose, and I had never seen her in such a good mood.

Percy started break dancing. We begged him not to—though

we wanted him to—and when he did dance, it was pretty impressive, and Natalie and I started cheering him on. Then Sarah Shay spilled some punch on me. It mostly got on my pants.

"Hey!" I said. "You did that on purpose!"

"You can't prove that!"

We were yelling because we were so close to the speakers.

Just a little bit after that, Bess Eberlee did the same thing. I guess it was one way to jab at me if I hadn't picked you as my date. Go ahead, dump punch on me. Dump away, girls. I can take it.

Penelope and I left the dance floor. We needed a breather and we went up the grass slope a little bit and from there we had a nice view of the whole shebang. I let Penelope sit on my tuxedo coat and while we sat there, she undid her French braid.

"It's a feeling that's familiar to me somehow," I said.

"What is?"

"Being here. Being at prom."

We looked down on the party. Penelope was still working on her hair. She got the braid undone and then she stood up and bent over so that her hair hung down and she combed it out with her fingers and then she stood up, flipping her hair back. She sat back down.

She said, "It's kind of like recess, prom is."

She was right. I definitely had that recess feeling. It was a feeling I hadn't felt in years.

I wasn't getting tired. Not in the least. We had been here an hour and a half and if anything I was more energized than I had been when we'd arrived. Dancing with Mrs. K. and countless others hadn't worn me out. Talking to Mrs. K. and Kaylee and Penelope and the principal and Laura Schiller and Jenny Wester and some-one from the yearbook and someone from the newspaper and Vance Mohr from homeroom and Patrick Kilmadden from English and Mrs. Derrywood and Shawn Brockmeier and Hannah Franz and countless others had not worn me out.

Mrs. K. and I left and I drove her home and walked her to her door. She took my hand at the door and held it between both of hers.

"Jack," she said, "you have such a big heart and I want you to know that you have made me and Mr. Kowalski very happy."

I felt my eyes getting a little moist. "That's okay," was all I could manage. I patted her top hand.

"Come in for a second," she said. "There's something I want to give you."

We went inside and I waited in the living room. The house was so quiet compared to the prom. Mrs. K. went down the hall-way to her bedroom and soon returned with a little box, which she handed to me.

"Go on," she said.

There were silver cuff links in the box.

"They're Mr. K.'s and he always wore them to the prom and I want you to take them. Wear them for the rest of the night, and then keep them."

"Oh, Mrs. K., I couldn't do that, but thank you. That's so sweet."

"No," she said. "He and I talked about it, and he wants you to have them. It's all settled."

I looked at the cuff links again.

"And I'll tell you something else about them," she said. "He was wearing those the night we met, fifty years ago."

I walked back to the car—Mr. K. had told me to keep the car all night—and I got in and sat there. I was full of things I wanted to say, things I wanted to do, people I wanted to be with, places I wanted to visit. I would return to the prom soon, but right now I had an errand to run. I had to see someone.

I drove up Kirkwood, up Summit, west on Market, north on Dubuque, west on Park Road. I turned left and wound my way up the hill. In the street I could see huge, sloppy, spray-painted letters that read I'M SORRY, NA. I stopped in front of Natalie's mother's house. There were lights on somewhere at the back of the house. I rang the bell. After a long time Bridget opened the door. She was just wearing jeans and a T-shirt and she was barefoot.

"So . . ." I said. "I, for one, feel like soft ice cream."

"Hey, you," she said. She looked behind me. "Where's everybody else?"

"Still at the party," I said. "I just took Mrs. K. home, and then I was thinking, I feel like soft ice cream. Now, don't I know someone else who likes soft ice cream? 'Cause I sure feel like soft ice cream."

She poked me. "You don't feel like soft ice cream," she said. "You just feel like a person."

I poked myself. "I see what you're saying. But you've gotta trust me: on the *inside* I feel like soft ice cream."

"Gross," she said.

"That is kind of gross. My apologies."

"And aren't you full of cheap cake and so forth?"

"You wouldn't believe how bad the cake was," I said. "Only ate one bite."

"One bite?"

"If that. I swear."

Bridget and Natalie's mom was actually a chaperone at the prom—I'd talked to her for a good five minutes at the reception table—so we didn't even have to ask permission for Bridget to leave the house. We simply made a pact that we'd never even tell anyone that it had happened.

The next stop on our soft ice-cream quest was Dane's Drive-In, just off Highway 1 on the southwest side of town. We pulled up in the Cadillac and debated whether we should go through the drive-through or walk up to the window. The drive-through offered the advantage of showing off the car, whereas walking up offered the advantage of showing off my tuxedo.

"How 'bout," Bridget said, "we walk up, order, then eat in the car. That's the best of both worlds."

It was a good decision, and we wowed them with the tux and then took our small swirl cones to the car and then I had second thoughts on account of it not being my car and not wanting to drip ice cream onto the seats. So we sat on the trunk, staring across the vacant parking lot at the bright signs of Vic's Auto Body, and we licked and licked and licked, and we agreed whole-heartedly that not only was this better than Dairy Queen, it was also better than the ice-cream place we'd been to in Tiffin just a few days ago. We munched our cones down to nubbins, then ate that final creamy-crunchy mouthful in unison.

Then, while she was still chewing, I said, "I do adore you, FancyPants."

She kept chewing, then swallowed and smiled a little. "What?"

"You're FancyPants," I said.

"Is this a trick you try on all the girls, trying to flush out FancyPants?"

"No, because I didn't figure it out until last night. I didn't piece it together."

She nodded. She looked at her lap. She looked at the ground.

"I'm really happy it's you," I said.

"This is embarrassing," she said.

"There's nothing to be embarrassed about," I said. "The stuff you said to me, wrote to me, it all helped me. It was all brilliant. You helped me a lot. And you helped me uncover that stupid conspiracy."

"But I also confused you," she said. "I confused you by sending mixed messages and being mysterious and hiding."

"True," I said. "But so what? You didn't mean to toy with me, even if that's what you did."

She shrugged. "There's grass on your jacket," she said.

I brushed my shoulder.

"But tell me," I said, "how'd you get to be so *wise*? Your e-mails read like something written by someone twice your age."

"I don't know," she said. "But I do take Flintstone vitamins every day."

"Must help," I said.

"Oh, they're very good for you."

"Maybe you can help me out now," I said. "Maybe you have some more advice for me, because I have to admit that I'm kind of at a loss at this precise moment. There's this girl I like—this fabulous, cute, funny, way-too-smart girl. And I'm pretty much gaga over this girl, I'm pretty much a lost cause. I'm ass over teakettle for this girl. She helped talk me through a tough week— the toughest week of my life. She's great at pinball, she's a mean Ping-Pong player, and she's just better than me in almost every way. And she's mature and I've seen some of her extremely impressive woodworking projects and the word on the street is that she's turning into one of the best shooting guards on the basketball team. And when I think of her, she crowds out girls like Pamela Brown. She just crowds them right out of my mind because that's how fantastic she is. That's how much she means to me. And if this girl were, say, four or five years older, then, well, then I wouldn't be asking what I should do because I would *know* what I should do. If she were five years older, I'd just plain fall in love with her. Blamo. Just like that. That's what I'd do. But she's not four or five years older, and I'm not four or five years younger, and therein is my dilemma, or at least the crux of it." I sighed. I rubbed my hands together. "Anyhoo," I said, "maybe you can help me. Maybe you know what to do."

She was sitting there, looking down. She had listened to everything. She had heard it all. She was absorbing it. Finally she looked across the empty parking lot, then looked up at the sky— which was half clouds, half stars.

"I don't know," she said.

"Me either," I said. "Not a clue." I scratched my face. "Well . . ." I said. "I mean, I have some *ideas* . . . . Nothing concrete, just some ideas. Like she and I could continue our ice-cream quest."

"Yeah."

"And she could help me become a better pinball player," I said.

"That wouldn't be hard."

"And when summer comes, maybe she and I and Nat and whoever else wants to come could go swimming out at Kent Park."

She nodded. "Maybe a bunch of us could catch a few movies this summer," she said. "A few blockbuster pieces of crap."

"Agreed," I said. "I pledge to see a minimum of four blockbuster pieces of crap with her between Memorial Day and . . . and . . ."

"And whenever you leave for college," she finished for me.

"Perfect," I said. "And you know I have this tux rented for a week, so perhaps a whole bunch of us should go bowling in formal wear next week."

"I don't have any formal wear."

"Then it could be formal wear optional."

"Okay."

We didn't talk for a little bit. Behind us, the lights at the ice-cream stand were buzzing. It was after eleven. A small plane swung low over the city, right to left, coming in for a landing at the airport behind us.

"So how'd you figure it out?" she asked in the car. "That I was FancyPants?"

"Little pieces, here and there. Like the fact that once after IMing with you, I tried to call Natalie and the voice mail picked up immediately because you were online with me. Or the fact that you seemed to know so much stuff about me. But when it really happened, when it really clicked, was last night when I was sitting there in Country Kitchen dealing with the Natalie and

Percy conspiracy and you said to me that it was my own life and that I would have to answer my own questions, well, when you said that, I heard FancyPants. And it made sense. You had obviously overheard Natalie doing some of her behind-the-scene rigging, which is why you tried to warn me about it early on."

"I tried to learn more so that I could help you."

"You did more than enough."

"I mucked things up," she said. "If it hadn't been for me, maybe you would have picked someone tonight."

"Maybe," I said. "Maybe. But that doesn't mean I'd be having more fun than I am. And besides, the truth about Natalie and Percy's plan would have come out eventually."

"So then what's the verdict? How do you feel after having lived through this week?"

"I don't know for sure," I said. "Maybe I just know myself a little bit better."

"Oh, good answer."

"Maybe I'm not as intimidated by the world, by people. The worst thing that people can really do is say 'no' to you. And 'no' isn't that bad because eventually it helps point you in the right direction, I think. Helps you find 'yes.'"

"I like that," she said.

We agreed never to tell anyone that she was FancyPants.

chapter 31

BACK AT THE PROM, the hour wore on. I wandered for a little while, feeling a bit adrift, but happily so. Scott Brader ambushed me and gave me an uncomfortable waist-level hug from his wheelchair. He was excited because while I'd been gone, he'd been crowned prom king.

"I didn't even know you could be a candidate if you had a broken ankle!" he exclaimed.

"I guess it's a very egalitarian system," I said.

"Egal-uh-what?" he said.

"So you two are the happy royal couple?" I said. "That makes me feel pretty good since I helped get you here together."

"Oh, but . . ." he said.

"What?"

"Kaylee isn't the queen."

"Oops."

"Ah, she'll be okay. She'll mope it off."

"Maybe you should go talk to her," I prompted.

He nodded. "You're right."

"Maybe you could present your beautiful prom king crown to her."

He thought that was about the best idea he had ever heard.

There was a breeze playing across the football field, and the dance floor was crowded—overflowing, actually—and the lines for the three dinky carnival rides—a carousel, a kiddie roller coaster, and a spinning teacup sort of thing—were growing. People recognized me and greeted me. The mood was high, and I felt like I belonged here. Suddenly I saw Natalie dancing by herself in the grass at the edge of the dance floor. Her eyes were closed, and she was holding her shoes in her hands. She was barefoot, like her sister. I watched her and wondered. I thought maybe I should leave her alone.

But I didn't. I walked over to her.

"Hey," I said when I was standing right in front of her.

She opened her eyes and stopped dancing. We just stood there, with people dancing around us. After a couple of moments she took my arm, and we walked away from the dance floor.

"You were gone so long," she said.

"I'm sorry," I said. "That Mrs. K. is a talker."

We sat at the bottom of the bleachers. Natalie tucked her legs under her. She looked at me, then she looked around at the prom. "I don't know where everyone else is," she said. "I saw Percy a while ago with a giant foam cowboy hat on. I think he won it in the raffle. And Dan is over talking to a bunch of baseball people, which just bores the heck out of me. I saw Sarah Shay up by the . . ."

She trailed off and looked at me. I was sitting with my

head down, and she lifted my chin and two tears ran down my cheeks.

"Jack? What?" Natalie said. "What is it?"

I wiped my face with my sleeve. "It's nothing," I said.

"No, it isn't," she said.

"Are we still friends?" I asked.

She looked at me, right in the eyes. She took my hands. "Of course we are," she said.

I was still crying, and my sleeve was just rubbing the tears everywhere.

"We *are*," she said.

"It felt like maybe we weren't," I said. "Maybe things had gotten too weird in there."

"Oh, Jack," she said, putting her arms around me. "How could we not be friends? How is that even possible? It's not. Not at all. Even if we're pissed off at each other every once in a while, we're still friends."

I smiled. I sighed. I smiled again and wiped my eyes. "I was just worried," I said. "Ever since, ever since . . . I just didn't know how things stood between us."

"Okay, so we hit a bump this week. But so what? Remember when I was going out with Greg Porter and you didn't talk to me for two months because you thought he was such an asshole? We got over that."

"Well, but I was *right*."

"True."

"And in this case, I don't know who's right or wrong."

"There's no blame to assign here," she said.

"I guess," I said. The tears had stopped. My face was cold and I was shivering a little bit and Natalie held me tighter. "Partly it's that things are changing," I said. "In a few weeks school will be over, we'll be graduating, we'll be moving on."

"I know," she said.

"I've known you for six years," I said.

"You're going to know me for a lot longer," she said. "We're going to know each other forever."

I nodded.

"And Percy, too," she added.

We sat looking out at the prom.

"We're very young, aren't we," she said after a while. "We really are. We don't know what's going to happen. Maybe what happened to us this week is like a grain of sand that gets stuck inside an oyster and over time it becomes a pearl. We don't know. Or maybe . . . maybe . . ."

"Maybe it's just a grain of sand," I said.

"Maybe," she conceded. "But that's not *bad*."

"No," I said. "I like sand. Usually."

"Sand is pretty cool," she agreed.

"Yeah," I said.

"Yep."

"Glass is made of sand," I said.

"Sure is."

We sat there. Then we laughed. Natalie jogged over to one of the refreshment tents and got me a cup of punch. I drank it all. She scooted herself next to me and then leaned her head on my shoulder.

"I wonder what's going to happen *next* week," I said.

"No way to tell," she said. "You had a big week."

"Actually, I'm kind of excited about it. About next week, and the week after, and the week after that, and so on. I feel like I can see things pretty clearly right now. I learned how to see things pretty clearly."

"That's a valuable thing," she said.

After a while we agreed to get back to the prom. I asked her if she'd been on the carousel yet. She hadn't, so we headed over there and stood at the back of the line, and as we waited, the wind started kicking up and Natalie screamed gleefully as her hair was whipped back and forth, and suddenly, as if from nowhere, it was raining—raining hard. Everyone in the line for the carousel rushed forward and crowded onto it to get out of the rain—the tents were too far away. The carousel kept turning, and the crowd separated me and Natalie, and the lights inside the carousel were golden and bright, and the music was lost behind the hubbub of the crowd and the whoosh of the downpour on the roof.

More people kept crowding onto the carousel, and I was getting pushed farther and farther toward the center. I was looking for Natalie and I was slightly dizzy because we were still spinning and I was stepping backward when I stepped on something uneven and I slipped and fell backward, only to be caught in the arms of the girl behind me.

"Sorry," I said, "I . . ."

The girl who had caught me was Adrian Swift. Well, at least this time I wasn't kissing someone.

"I—I . . ." I stammered, getting back to my feet.

"Yes?" she said.

"I . . ."

She was looking right into me. I smiled.

"I think I owe you an explanation."

"You don't," she said.

"Or about six explanations," I said.

"It's okay, really."

"Humor me," I said. "Please."

She nodded. My stomach had clenched up, but I wanted to do this. I wanted to deal with her honestly.

"Um, where to start? Well, that day when you approached me, I had this, I was, I . . . I . . . I was pretty darn sick, you see, and I just didn't even want to go to prom and so I just lied to you and . . ."

"And?"

I threw up my hands. The crowd pushed Adrian and me closer together.

"I'm a bad, bad person," I said. "I apologize. When you saw me with Julie and later with Pamela Brown—"

"And Natalie."

"Right."

"And Mrs. Kowalski."

"Right, well, I wanted to explain to you."

"It's all right," she said. "You're allowed to date whoever you want."

"True, but I lied to you, and that's what I'm apologizing for."

"I appreciate that," she said.

"And I never had rickets and I never meant to say that, but there was no way to recover from it and last spring I went to all the Knowledge Bowl matches because you were in them."

"I see," she said.

"Wait, did I just say that?"

"I think you did."

We stood close together in the throng of people. The rain wasn't letting up.

"Who are you here with?" I asked.

"Myself," she said.

"This is going to put a damper on things real quick," I said, pointing up, indicating the rain.

She nodded. She told me that she'd seen me dance with Mrs. K. and that she thought it was a nice thing to do, what with Mr. K. in the hospital, and she asked me how I learned how to dance.

"When my sister got married four years ago, my mom and sister and I all took dancing lessons together."

"Really? That's pretty cool."

"It's actually pretty dorky."

"Well, when I say cool, you have to understand that I mean dorky."

"I can dig that," I said. "And when I say pretty dorky, I mean really dorky. And when I say really dorky, I mean me."

"We should have a dork contest."

"Don't even start with me. You don't want to get into a dork contest with me."

"Maybe later, then?" she said.

"Just consider yourself warned. Consider yourself duly notified," I said.

She smiled. "We're going to the same college, you know."

"Who? What do you mean?"

"Me and you, we're going to the same college."

"We are? I didn't know anyone else from City High was going there! That's amazing."

We talked a little bit about college. We'd both heard some of the same rumors. We'd both signed up for the early orientation. We'd both requested the same dorm. As we talked, I found myself wanting to know more and more about her. She was plainspoken, not sarcastic or cool or egotistical. She didn't have any odd piercings, and she didn't have a fifty-dollar haircut. Far from it, actually: her hair was unruly and kind of bushy, but I adored it. And she kept trying to tuck her hair behind her ear as we talked, but it kept springing free. I noticed that her earrings were tiny butterflies. Really, she reminded me of my sisters.

The crowd on the carousel was getting louder, the rain was coming straight down, heavy as ever, and my stomach growled despite my recent ice-cream run.

"Is that your stomach?" Adrian said, interrupting what I was saying.

"You heard that?" I asked. "Cripes."

"Are you hungry?"

"I guess so. I didn't eat much at dinner. Too excited." Somehow the ice cream I'd eaten an hour ago had only made me hungrier.

"Me either," she said. "And the cake here was inedible."

We stood there.

"Inedible?" I said. "It was like sugared clay or something."

"Sugared clay?"

"Yeah. Hey, do you . . ." I said. "Do you want to go get something to eat? Do you want to go to Country Kitchen? Eat some midnight breakfast? Drink some so-so coffee?"

"Right now?"

"Yeah, I mean, if you don't have plans."

"I was supposed to go to Bobby Berringer's post-prom, but that sounds like my idea of purgatory."

"Like purgatory, but without the chance of ever actually getting into heaven," I said.

She said, "Then let's skip it together."

We wormed our way to the outer edge of the carousel platform. The rain was formidable, and we stood there before taking the plunge. I felt giddy. I felt different. I had just asked out a girl on the spur of the moment. I'd never really done that before. But it felt fine.

"Afraid of water?" she asked. And she stepped off into the rain.

I followed her, but I immediately thought of a snag in our plans. What were the logistics? Did she have a car? Could I take the Caddy? I'd have to tell Percy—he was counting on the ride.

"Wait," I said. We stopped in the rain. "Do you have a car here?"

"Yeah, I can drive us," she said. I admired that she wasn't afraid of the rain. There we were, getting soaked, and she wasn't whining about her hair or her dress or anything.

"Then I have to give my car keys to my friend," I said, "and I don't know how the heck we're going to find him in this place."

"You mean him?" Adrian asked, and she pointed back at the carousel, and there was Percy, tuxedo jacket long gone, red foam cowboy hat held aloft as he rode one of the carousel's horses like a bucking bronco. Penelope was on the horse with him.

"Percy!" I called, and he saw me.

"Buddy!" he said. He was rotating out of sight, so I jogged to keep up with him. "Why are you in the rain? Climb aboard the Starship Tomorrowland!"

"This thing just happened," I said. Why was I struggling for words?

"What thing?"

"I don't know, I don't know," I said, jogging along. "I mean, I just met someone."

"Congratulations," he said.

"Did you say you met someone?" Penelope said.

"Yes, and I don't know for sure, but I've got this feeling about her, and . . . and . . . I don't really know how to explain it."

"Don't explain it," Percy said. "Just go with it."

"You're right," I said.

"Why are you here telling me when you should be off with her?" Percy asked.

"Oh, because we're leaving in her car, so I needed to tell you that the Cadillac is yours."

"Gotchya. Message received. Now go!"

I waved and veered off from my course only to run smack into Adrian. I had run one full circuit of the carousel and come right back to where I'd started.

"Ready, then?" she asked.

"Sorry about the collision," I said.

"Maybe we should head for the car," she said. "It's raining narder."

So we started walking away. But we hadn't gone far when I stopped.

"Wait!" I called. "I've got to give him the keys. Why am I such a spaz?"

"There he comes," she said, looking back at the carousel.

Indeed, there he was, and both he and Penelope were looking at us, trying to see who I was with. I pulled the keys out of my pocket and I held them up and he held out his hand and I hesitated.

"You can do it," Adrian said.

And then, in what was one of the most challenging throws of my young life, I sent the keys flying toward my cowboy friend. They arced through the night, through the rain, sparkling in mid-air, and all eyes were on them—everyone in that section of the carousel was following this little drama—and they flew straight and true, as if guided, and Percy plucked them from their flight with one hand and gave a mighty cowboy, "Yee-ha!"

The crowd cheered loudly and then Percy rotated smoothly out of sight. The cheering faded.

"Impressive," I said. "That was a good throw."

"If you don't say so yourself," Adrian said. "Now can we run?"

I looked at her. Water was streaming down her face. "But how can you run in heels?" I asked.

"Heels?" she said. "I think not." And she lifted the hem of her dress and we both looked down. She was wearing running shoes.

"Oh, wow," I said.

"Now," she said, "can you keep up?"